T0010110

Hannah sucked

Oh God.

She was still cavorting around in her bra and panties. In front of Alden. Where had she thrown her dress off? Or maybe Alden had taken it off her. That thought had heat rushing to her cheeks.

Luckily, Alden distracted her by locating her dress. She thanked him and quickly threw it on.

"You're welcome," he answered.

Hannah was sorely tempted to just crawl back into bed and forget any of this was even happening.

To be oblivious again to reality, as she'd been just a few minutes earlier. When she'd been snuggled close and warm in Alden's arms.

"We absolutely can't mention any of this to anyone."

He nodded. "Agreed."

"Thank you," she said.

He shrugged and smiled at her with a playful wink. For a split second, the sheer beauty that was Alden Hamid served to take her breath away and she could easily see why she would have pledged to marry him with eager enthusiasm.

"You're welcome," he answered. "It's what any decent husband would do."

Dear Reader,

The concept of family means different things to different people. I'm always so fascinated by the individual interpretations I come across. Alden Hamid and Hannah Devine grew up in very different households. She was raised by a single mother, one who was often overbearing and demanding. Alden, in turn, was abandoned by both parents. Each has detrimental ideas about how they can contribute to any kind of family unit given the examples they lived themselves.

But then fate throws them together again after several years apart. Then somehow they end up accidentally married!

What follows is an adventurous journey through several exotic locations.

Along the way, they learn just how meant for each other they have been all along.

And discover the found family they both deserve and will forever cherish. With each other.

I hope you enjoy their story.

Nina Singh

THEIR ACCIDENTAL MARRIAGE DEAL

NINA SINGH

Harlequin

ROMANCE

If you purchased this book without a cover you should be aware that this book is stolen property. It was reported as "unsold and destroyed" to the publisher, and neither the author nor the publisher has received any payment for this "stripped book."

Harlequin®
ROMANCE

ISBN-13: 978-1-335-59672-7

Their Accidental Marriage Deal

Copyright © 2024 by Nilay Nina Singh

Recycling programs for this product may not exist in your area.

All rights reserved. No part of this book may be used or reproduced in any manner whatsoever without written permission.

Without limiting the author's and publisher's exclusive rights, any unauthorized use of this publication to train generative artificial intelligence (AI) technologies is expressly prohibited.

This is a work of fiction. Names, characters, places and incidents are either the product of the author's imagination or are used fictitiously. Any resemblance to actual persons, living or dead, businesses, companies, events or locales is entirely coincidental.

For questions and comments about the quality of this book, please contact us at CustomerService@Harlequin.com.

TM and ® are trademarks of Harlequin Enterprises ULC.

 Harlequin Enterprises ULC
22 Adelaide St. West, 41st Floor
Toronto, Ontario M5H 4E3, Canada
www.Harlequin.com

Printed in U.S.A.

Nina Singh lives just outside Boston, Massachusetts, with her husband, children and a very rambunctious Yorkie. After several years in the corporate world, she finally followed the advice of family and friends to "give the writing a go, already." She's oh-so-happy she did. When not at her keyboard, she likes to spend time on the tennis court or golf course. Or immersed in a good read.

Books by Nina Singh

Harlequin Romance

A Five-Star Family Reunion
Wearing His Ring till Christmas

How to Make a Wedding
From Tropical Fling to Forever

Spanish Tycoon's Convenient Bride
Her Inconvenient Christmas Reunion
From Wedding Fling to Baby Surprise
Around the World with the Millionaire
Whisked into the Billionaire's World
Caribbean Contract with Her Boss
Two Weeks to Tempt the Tycoon
The Prince's Safari Temptation
Part of His Royal World

Visit the Author Profile page
at Harlequin.com for more titles.

To my parents

**Praise for
Nina Singh**

"A captivating holiday adventure!
Their Festive Island Escape by Nina Singh is a twist
on an enemies-to-lovers trope and is sure to delight.
I recommend this book to anyone.... It's fun,
it's touching and it's satisfying."

—*Goodreads*

CHAPTER ONE

HANNAH DEVINE WALKED into the pre-wedding celebration party, all the while cursing the life decisions that had brought her to this moment. This utterly, astoundingly, shatteringly humiliating moment. She had to be the only one attending these events solo. There was no doubt about it. No one else she'd gone to high school with would be pathetic enough to find themselves in such a predicament: attending the wedding of the most devoted couple in their class sans a plus-one.

The infuriating thing was she'd had a plus-one up until about a short seventy-two hours ago. Then she'd been unceremoniously dumped. By none other than the man she'd thought would be her own groom.

Ha! What a joke of an idea that was apparently.

The rooftop of the luxury Vegas resort was decorated like a tropical island. Complete with faux palm trees adorned with hanging plastic coconuts. Pictures of Max and Mandy decorated every flat surface.

She'd come this close to canceling, feigning illness or some kind of schedule conflict. But in the end, her pride had run out. After all, the reality of her broken relationship would reach the proverbial gossip vine soon enough. So she'd shown up to deliver the news herself to anyone who asked.

Hannah took a deep breath, summoned the will to pull herself out of the self-defeating thoughts. This week wasn't about her. She was here to watch Mandy and Max get married. M and M as they were called during their teen years. Reardon High's golden couple.

Honestly, it was rather surprising that the two of them waited this long before tying the knot. But maybe Hannah was naive about the realities of matrimony and love. After all, look at the state of her own romantic life.

Or lack thereof to be more accurate.

How could she have not even seen it coming? Justin had claimed she was oblivious to his moods and desires more than once. Turned out he was right. Because she'd really thought that this weekend would be her own step toward an official engagement. She'd actually thought Justin might propose given the romantic reason for this trip to Las Vegas. Instead, things had gone completely the opposite way than she'd anticipated. Rather than be swayed in any way, he'd said the idea of even attending a wedding made him realize just how unready he felt to take any such step himself.

He'd even tried to placate her with the "it's not you, it's me" garbage line. Except that wasn't very convincing. It had to be her to some degree, didn't it?

Hannah gave a brisk shake of her head and made her way toward the crowded open bar. Not as if any of those questions mattered. The simple fact was that she'd be attending this weekend's events solo. Starting with this outdoor reggae-themed party poolside at one of Las Vegas's most swanky hotel slash casinos.

She wasn't usually much of a drinker.

But she was going to need some liquid fortitude to get through the next several hours as all the questions rained down about why she was here without her plus-one.

Though usually being a non-imbiber, she wasn't even sure where to start. What should she even order? Justin had insisted she join him as a devoted teetotaler. Alcohol was strictly off limits as far as her ex was concerned, even at special occasions. He was much too concerned about being in full control of himself at all times. Not acceptable to allow anything that would facilitate the lowering of inhibitions. Their nightly ritual consisted of Hannah brewing a small pot of tea, usually something herbal. The only times she'd allowed herself to indulge was when she'd been out with girlfriends. And then, if Justin got wind of her indulgence, he'd be sure to make his displeasure known. The following day would be spent in cold silence with hardly a word spoken between them until she'd made some kind of gesture to make amends.

Hannah gave herself a mental forehead thwack. This weekend was going to be utter torture if she insisted on rehashing the details of her now-defunct relationship.

But there was something else on her mind, or someone more accurately. Thoughts of him had been scrambling around in her brain ever since the invitation had arrived. She had no doubt that Alden would be invited to the wedding. The question was would he come?

The answer came soon enough.

She sensed him behind her before she even saw him.

Alden Hamid had a way of shifting the entire aura of an area as soon as he arrived in a space. Or maybe that was just the way she'd always reacted to him.

Funny how that hadn't changed after all these years. And now she was single... Hannah gave her head a brisk shake to knock that thought right out of her head. That line of thinking could lead nowhere good. She'd been down that road before when she was much younger and even more naive. No, where Alden Hamid was concerned, she'd do well to remember all the reasons she needed to stay clear of the man and protect her heart as far as men like him were concerned. And that man in particular.

Still, yet another wayward thought crept into her head. Had he noticed her?

Highly unlikely. Especially considering a swarm of their female former classmates had immediately rushed to his side as soon as he appeared, Hannah saw when she risked a side-eye glance his way. Not that she could blame said classmates. Even from this distance, she could see clearly that Alden hadn't lost any of his women-magnet, drop-dead gorgeous looks.

No, if anything, Alden was even better looking now. He'd grown into his features. His jaw was more chiseled. His cheekbones edgier. The man himself appeared edgier.

If she were bolder, she might have approached him as well. But she'd never been that bold.

A throaty feminine voice broke through her

thoughts. "Here. You look like you could use this."

Hannah looked up to find a petite brunette holding a serving tray, offering her a frosty goblet of a sugar-rimmed drink. She took the offering with gratitude and downed a large gulp before thanking the server whose name tag said *Elise*.

"Is it that obvious?"

Elise nodded with a pleasant smile.

Hannah returned it with a sheepish one of her own. "Sorry, I haven't seen some of these people in several years. It's a bit overwhelming to be amongst all my old high school mates again."

Elise's gaze followed where Hannah's had been a moment ago.

"Friend of yours?" Elise asked, then quirked an eyebrow when Hannah didn't answer right away.

"It's…complicated," she finally offered. She wouldn't even begin to know how to explain her and Alden's relationship back when they'd both been teens. Sure, she supposed they'd been friends. But they would have never spent a moment in each other's company if Hannah's best friend hadn't been dating Alden's best buddy. The very bride and groom.

"I see. That's him then, is it?" Elise asked.

"I'm sorry?"

"He's clearly the one everyone's been curious to see again. I'd venture he was the big man on campus? The one all the cheerleaders and chess club geniuses alike swooned over?"

Hannah tapped her finger to her forehead in a mock salute. "Very perceptive of you, Elise. You are one hundred percent on the nose correct. How did you know?"

It was a rhetorical question.

He really shouldn't have come.

If the groom were anyone but Max, one of the very few people in this world who'd ever given a care for him, Alden would have steered clear of any wedding by miles and miles.

He'd only just gotten here and already the memories were swarming his brain. Memories involving one person in particular.

He'd spotted her just as she turned his way. There she was. The girl that got away. Or, to be more accurate, the one he'd never actually had a chance with in the first place.

He and Hannah Devine had attended more than a few events with each other, had hung out together on several occasions during their teen years. But never just the two of them. And never alone. They'd simply been the couple tagging along to provide the second part of the double date. Alden had never been able to figure out if Max kept asking him to accompany him and Mandy out of a real desire to spend time in a group or because his friend had felt genuinely sorry for him. Most likely, it was the latter.

Now, here they all were. With one half of that foursome about to finally tie the knot. And the other half throwing awkward glances at each other across a rooftop bar.

Despite not having seen her as anything other than an online thumbnail on the Boston business sites, he had no trouble recognizing Hannah the instant his eyes landed on her. Not that there weren't subtle differences. Gone was the tight ponytail. She now wore her hair in loose curls that fell around her face and shoulders. Her facial features more angular and womanlike.

A feminine shriek of laughter sounded behind him, pulling him out of his thoughts. He turned to find the source of the noise approaching him, arms outstretched and flashing a wide smile.

The woman looked familiar in a distant way, enough to let him know they'd been in the same biology class back in high school. But damned if he could recall her name. Or anything else about her, for that matter.

Amy? Alison? Ariel?

Alden's mind scrambled to recall but it was no use. Whoever she was, she embraced him in a tight bear hug as soon as she reached his side.

"How have you been?" she wanted to know once she finally let go.

Alden reflexively glanced in Hannah's direction before trying to come up with an answer. But Hannah was no longer in the same spot. Where had she gone? A sinking feeling hit in the center of his gut at the thought that she might have already left the party. Not that he'd had any intention of actually speaking with her aside from a quick hello. What would he possibly say?

Then again, he'd never really known what to say to Hannah. Some things never changed.

"Alden? You in there?" the woman in front of him asked in a light tone, yet he detected a slight hint of annoyance in her voice. He forced his attention back to her face and pulled a smile. Still had no clue who she was but he could hold a generic enough conversation without letting on. He was good at faking such things.

He'd had lots of practice.

What was this woman's name? For the life of him, the answer wasn't clicking in his brain. Plus, he had to admit, he didn't really care that much. Other than being polite, he had no interest in any of the people here. Well, aside from the bridal couple and one other.

"You don't remember me, do you?" the woman asked.

Alden was scrambling for a way to admit the truth of her words when his gaze was drawn to the person approaching from the opposite side. His brain instantly registered who it was. Hannah.

But it wasn't him she stepped up to when she reached his side.

"Alyssa Cambell. Is that you?" Hannah asked the other woman, a wide smile plastered on her face.

Huh. So that's who she was. The Reardon High Wildcats' lead cheerleader for most of their high school years. Lead cheerleader and head of the most exclusive clique. No wonder she'd been so perturbed that he hadn't remembered her. Back in school, everyone knew who Alyssa Cambell was.

Alyssa turned to face Hannah, blinking in clear confusion and irritation. She didn't seem to appreciate the intrusion.

"Hello," Alyssa answered. "And you are? I don't seem to remember you," she added without so much as a hint of apology.

"Hannah Devine. We were in the same calculus class. I tutored you before finals that year."

It was clear Alyssa wasn't listening. Her attention had moved to another focal point.

"Excuse me," she said dismissively after a few short beats. "I see someone I'd like to talk to." Without waiting for an answer, from either one of them, she turned and walked away. Leaving him and Hannah staring at each other in awkward silence.

Alden cleared his throat. "That was for my benefit, wasn't it? Did I look that uncomfortable?"

She smiled at him with a small shrug. "You did actually."

He gave her a small bow. "Well, thank you for coming so helpfully to my rescue. For the life of me, I couldn't remember who she was."

"You're probably the only one."

"I know exactly who you are, however," he blurted out without thinking. Now why had he gone and said that? That sounded like he might have been thinking about her through the years. As if perhaps she'd been ingrained in his memory even after all this time. Like he'd scanned the business sections of websites and newspapers related to a city he hadn't even visited since moving out of Massachusetts. All to catch snippets of information without having to actually follow her on social media.

"I remember you too, Alden." she said simply.

"I would ask you how you've been but there's really no need."

"Oh, yeah? Why's that?"

She ducked her head somewhat sheepishly. "I've been seeing your name here and there. One success after another. Taking the hospitality world by storm."

Huh. Maybe he hadn't been the only one mining for information. Did that mean she was impressed? Or was she just being polite? Probably the latter.

"The papers and websites often exaggerate."

"Funny, I don't recall you being particularly modest back in school."

He had to laugh at that. Little did she know, Alden's confidence back in school had all been a front. A disguise.

Hannah held her hands up in front of his face, forming a square bracket with her fingers.

"What are you doing?"

She shrugged. "Trying to measure your head. Making sure it hasn't grown too big given all your business successes the past year."

Her teasing elicited yet another chuckle. Wait. Was he actually beginning to enjoy himself? Very unexpected. Especially considering the last forty-eight hours and how much he'd been dreading this whole affair.

"So tell me what you've been up to. Still good at calculus?" he asked her.

Hannah didn't get a chance to answer as a noisy commotion drew their attention. A roar of cheers and whistles erupted in the air. It appeared the bride and groom had arrived and were being met with enthusiastic applause.

Hannah turned in the couple's direction and he took the opportunity to study her. Not much had changed. She was still drop-dead gorgeous in an understated way. Thick wavy dark hair that fell in waves around her shoulders. A slanted nose above full ruby red lips that she hadn't bothered to adorn with lipstick or gloss. And those eyes. The woman had the most striking eyes. Even more striking now that she'd grown into her features.

Those thumbnails hadn't done her justice.

Hannah was one of those women who didn't necessarily draw a lot of attention. Until one took the time to have a really good look at her.

Alden had no doubt she didn't know just how pretty she was, and never had. But Hannah Devine was one of the most attractive girls to graduate from Reardon High.

He'd always thought so, anyway. And still did.

What in the world had she been thinking? Breaking into Alden and Alyssa's conversation that way? The truth was she hadn't been thinking at all. The drink must have gone to her head. She really should have built up a tolerance before coming to a boozy wedding in a city that was considered to be one of the party capitals of the world.

Alden had just looked so uncomfortable, as if he were looking for a way out of the conversation. She'd simply been helping an old friend out of what was clearly an awkward situation. Only now the awkwardness had shifted to sit between the two of them instead.

Her mind reeled to various flashbacks of the two of them all those years ago, how awkward the air between them would feel during those short stints when they'd found themselves alone together. Yet another thing that hadn't changed much over the years. Alden and Hannah had never quite known how to fill the silence whenever it was just the two of them alone.

Hannah sighed and took another sip of her drink, much smaller this time. At the least, she had to slow it down a bit. If she were being honest with herself, she'd have to admit another truth. That something about seeing him with Alyssa had set off a squirmy sensation in her middle. The other woman was as beautiful as she'd been in high school.

But now, here Hannah was, standing there trying to come up with something to say.

Alden pointed to the glass in her hand. "You're running low. Can I get you another?" he asked.

That was the last thing she needed. But the little devilish Hannah that sometimes appeared on her shoulder popped up to whisper loudly in her ear. *What's the point? May as well enjoy yourself. If you can't let loose at a good friend's wedding, after being dumped by your almost-fiancé, what better time?*

Good question.

"Sure, why not," she answered, defiantly tossing back the remaining liquid in her glass.

Alden left her side and returned within minutes with a fresh drink for her and a sweaty bottle of beer for himself. He handed her the glass, then clinked his bottle to hers in a salute.

"To old friends."

"Here, here," Hannah answered taking another small sip. Was it her imagination, or was this cocktail even stronger than the last? Maybe she should have started out with beer like Alden. Or wine. She glanced at him as he drew a deep gulp from his bottle.

Upon closer inspection, she saw he hadn't really changed all that much. Except somehow he was even more handsome than the athletic muscular boy she'd sometimes hung out with before graduation. The years had added a ruggedness to his good looks. His hair appeared darker, curlier than it had been when they'd been younger. Alden Hamid was an intriguing combination of Middle Eastern dark features with tanned olive skin and dark hair, offset by bluish-gray eyes and nearly blond lashes. Features he'd inherited from his father and mother respectively.

Had he brought a date? Maybe he was here with a girlfriend who was powdering her nose at the moment. If the gossip sites were to be believed, he wasn't often lacking female companionship. The truth was she'd done more than her fair share of googling his name over the years. Not that she'd ever admit it to anyone, least of all to the man himself. Though it had been a while. She'd resisted the urge for the past few months. Now she wished she knew a bit more, particularly about his romantic life. Though it really was none of her business.

"Are you here with someone?" she shocked herself by blurting out and asking. Of all the things to say. Not to mention it was probably a stupid question. Even if he was here at the wedding alone, chances were good he was involved with someone. How could someone like him not be? Successful, handsome, well-known. A catch by any and all definitions.

If Alden were at all surprised by such a direct question, he didn't show it. Simply taking another swig from his bottle, he shook his head. "No. Here by myself."

Well, that hardly told her anything. Was he seeing someone but she couldn't make it here? Was he in between girlfriends? What was the story?

Why in the world was she entertaining such thoughts, anyway? She'd only had her heart broken a mere three days ago. She had no business wondering about her former crush's romantic life.

"What about you?" he asked a moment later.

To her shock, a well of hurt erupted within her chest. So overwhelming that she couldn't find her voice enough to answer. Damn Justin. She wasn't supposed to be here alone. She was to have arrived with the man she'd planned to spend the rest of her life with. She was supposed to have been part of a paired couple, like so many of the other attendees milling about this party.

Her silence was apparently answer enough.

"Wanna talk about it?" Alden asked.

She shrugged. "Not much to say. I find myself unexpectedly at a crossroads."

Alden blew out a breath, ending on a low whistle. "Wow. That's pretty heavy."

He gently took her by the elbow and turned in the direction of the elevator. "Here, follow me."

"But what about Max and Mandy?"

"We'll get a chance to say hello to them later. They're busy with other guests, anyway."

Two minutes later, they'd exited the elevator on the lobby level of the hotel.

"Where are we going?"

"Just away for a bit."

"Away?"

He nodded, leading her past a towering marble statue in the center of the lobby to the revolving glass doors at the entrance.

"I don't know about you, but I'm not exactly in a social mood. Sounded like you maybe could also use a break from being around all those people too."

His words gave her pause for their accuracy. How had he managed to read her so well after only seeing her for the briefest of moments? She must not have hidden her emotions that effectively. Just as well Alden had swept her away out of the party, then. The last thing she wanted to do was bring down what was supposed to be a festive celebration of two people getting married.

But now she was outside alone with him. Just the two of them.

Knowing full well it was a bad idea, she took a rather large gulp of her cocktail for some more liquid courage as she followed him toward the large fountain in the center of the courtyard. Only fountain wasn't quite an accurate way to describe the structure. Several torrents of water shot straight up into the sky, each one as tall as the building itself. A subtle mist kissed the surface of her face.

"So, you're at a crossroads, huh?" Alden asked after taking another swallow of his beer.

"It's a long story," she lied. It wasn't really. And a fairly classic one at that. She'd misread her romantic relationship in a colossal fashion. And now she was attending a wedding solo. A wedding that may as well have been a high school reunion.

"Your turn now. Tell me why you wanted to leave the party," she said, sitting down on the stone barrier around the artificial pond of water.

He rubbed his forehead, resting one foot on the concrete and taking another swig of beer.

"I'm beyond tired. Had to travel here all night from the Aegean coast—the jet lag is starting to catch up to me. And I haven't slept a wink for over forty-eight hours. Not to mention, I'm beyond frustrated."

"Why's that?"

"A business deal that's not exactly falling into place no matter how hard I try. If the couple getting married weren't Max and Mandy, I wouldn't have even bothered to show."

Hannah released an uncharacteristic giggle at his words. Funny, Alden was echoing her own exact thoughts about attending this wedding.

He leaned toward her, smiling. His aftershave mingled with the moisture in the air and tickled her nose, a more mature scent than the drugstore variety he used to wear back when they were kids. No doubt several times more expensive. "What's so funny?"

Another giggle escaped her lips before she answered. "I had the same exact thoughts on my way over here."

He lifted his bottle in another toast. "Well, now that we're both here, I say we make the most of it and have ourselves a good time. How are you at blackjack?"

Ninety minutes later, the answer to that question was abundantly clear. Hannah was absolutely lousy at blackjack. So much so that Alden made her leave the table before she lost any more money.

"So now what?" Hannah asked, as a server delivered yet another drink. Had she just slurred

her words? She had to slow down on the cocktails. Even as she thought it, she took a large sip.

"Let's get some air," Alden said, gently leading her by the elbow out of the casino.

She had no idea what time it was. But Vegas
was still completely awake and fully lit. If anything, the street appeared even more crowded
than when they'd first entered the casino.

Alden led her to a nearby bench and sat her
down, then rested his foot next to her thigh,
draping his forearm over his bent knee.

"You are really bad at card games, Miss
Devine," he teased.

Hannah shrugged. The world was slightly
off-balance. She should probably find a way to
get a cup of coffee. One thing was certain—
she was absolutely done drinking for the night.
Maybe for the entire month.

"I've never really played before," she explained in her defense. Actually, she'd never
really gambled before, unless one counted the
occasional lottery ticket. "And certainly not in
a casino in Las Vegas," she added, then wondered aloud, "Why did Max and Mandy decide
to get married here again?"

"Something about a central location convenient to most of the guests traveling for the
wedding," Alden answered.

That made sense. "They're finally doing it, finally tying the knot. After all these years."

Alden nodded, an indulgent smile on his lips. "Looks like it."

A feminine shriek of laughter pierced the air as a giggling couple walked past. Before they'd gone more than a few feet past the bench, the man turned around with a wide grin. "Congratulate us," he yelled over to Hannah and Alden. "We just got married!"

Hannah watched as he picked the woman up and twirled her around. "Huh. Looks like everyone's getting married."

Alden tilted his head. "Easy to do in this city."

"I thought I'd be getting married soon too," Hannah blurted out, then realized she didn't really want to talk about Justin at the moment. She didn't even want to think about him.

"Come again?"

She ignored the question as yet another high school memory surfaced in her head. "Hey, remember that silly secret ballot that was going around our senior year?"

Alden simply gave her a puzzled look. She went on, "You know, where you had to choose who you would marry if you found yourself single at the ripe old age of twenty-five? If the other person was single too, of course." The memory made her chuckle. "Can you believe we thought twenty-five was old, back then?"

Alden returned her laugh. "Yeah, now I remember. Trisha Sayton was asking everybody."

Hannah leaned closer to him, hardly believing what she was about to admit. "I have a confession to make," she said in a low voice.

"What's that?"

"I picked you."

Alden didn't so much as move, just stared deeply into her eyes. "What a coincidence," he said finally, his voice low and gravelly. For several moments, Hannah simply let the words sink in. He couldn't mean what she thought he might mean. Maybe she hadn't heard him right. She did feel rather off-center at the moment.

"Huh?" she said, by way of asking for clarification.

"I picked you."

Hannah felt her mouth drop. "You did?"

He tapped her nose playfully. "Is that so hard to believe?"

He had no idea. She might never believe it. But why would he lie?

"Wouldn't it be funny if…" Alden didn't finish his sentence. But she could guess what he'd been about to say. As ridiculous as it was.

"That *would* be pretty funny," she agreed.

"Hilarious."

"We're both way past the age of twenty-five," she declared.

"And we're both still single."

"True. And we did make a pledge. Trisha Sayton made us sign our names and everything."

"A binding contract, I'd say."

Hannah shook her head in agreement. "A contract is a contract."

CHAPTER TWO

ALDEN DID HIS best to try and open his eyes but his lids didn't seem to want to budge. An achy pounding drummed at the crown of his head. His tongue felt like he'd been dining on desert sand. The sound ringing in his ears could best be described as combination screech and jackhammer.

Something was clearly wrong. Terribly, horribly wrong.

Yet, somehow it also felt beautifully right.

Because in addition to all those unpleasant sensations assaulting his senses at the moment, there was also a much lovelier one. A warmth curling against his side, the scent of roses hovering delicately in the air.

Roses. Hannah always smelled like a fresh bouquet of summer blooms.

His eyes finally flew open as a bolt of alarm shot through his gut. He'd dreamed he and Hannah were lying on the king-sized bed in the suite he'd checked into earlier this afternoon. They were both clad in nothing but their undergarments. The curse he bit out might have caused his former football teammates to blush. Sure enough, the warm, soft, nearly naked body snuggled up next to him in bed was none other than Hannah Devine herself. He repeated the curse word more loudly before he could stop himself.

What in the world had they done?

What happened next appeared to be transpiring in slow motion. Hannah opened her eyes, then turned to face him. The she bolted upright, clocking his chin with her scalp in the process and adding a fresh new layer of agony to his suffering.

"Oh, my God!"

Alden rubbed his chin, tried to take a calming breath. The layer of new stubble along his skin told him it was indeed morning. So that would mean they'd spent the night together. One way or another.

Hannah gasped, scrambled to a sitting position as she looked about the room. "Where am I? And what—" She didn't finish, threw her hand against her mouth instead. "I'm going to be sick."

He could only watch as she fled to the bathroom.

Alden did his best to drown out the noises

coming from behind the bathroom door. The ringing in his ears helped the effort. When she finally emerged, she looked about as green as he felt.

But his stomach sunk further when he caught sight of her expression. Beyond appearing physically unwell, Hannah looked shaken. Wide-eyed, mouth agape, she'd gone pale.

Alarm bells joined the screeching in his ears. Besides waking up next to him in his hotel suite, which, admittedly was rather unsettling given the circumstances, what could possibly have her so frenzied?

The answer to that question became clear when she lifted a shaky hand and approached him slowly from across the room. There, sparkling brightly in a ray of sun shining from the glass wall overlooking the Vegas skyline, sat a fat diamond on her ring finger.

"Alden?" Her voice came out in a shaky whisper so low he almost didn't hear her.

They were in Vegas, the elopement capital of the world. They'd spent the night together. And Hannah was sporting a diamond on her ring finger. One hell of a puzzle to piece together.

"All right. Let's not panic. I'm sure there's a logical and sensible explanation." He wasn't sure of any such thing but he was grasping at straws here.

"What happened last night?" Hannah wanted to know.

Then he remembered, the images flooding his mind. The two of them laughing as he kept adding game chips to her pile each time she lost at the blackjack table. The servers at the casino coming by time and time again with the complimentary drinks. He flinched at the last picture that popped into his mind. Him carrying her out of a brightly lit jewelry store and through the pastel-painted doorway of a small house next door. A house that looked suspiciously like it might be a twenty-four-hour chapel.

Hannah began to pace from one end of the bed to the other. Even now, with all that was happening, he couldn't help but appreciate the way she looked in her sensible tankini-style bra and matching silky boy shorts. The ensemble was more modest than many of the bathing suits he saw aboard a yacht or on the beach, but the way she filled it out had his mind traveling places it had no business going considering their current predicament.

Focus.

The pieces falling into place in his head were beginning to form a picture that had only one logical answer to Hannah's question. She had to be reaching the same conclusion. Hannah had always been a bright girl.

"Let's hope and pray we didn't actually go through with it," he said, rising up off the mattress and onto legs that were less than steady.

Even as he spoke the words, his eye caught a piece of paper lying on the floor near his discarded shirt and pants. An official-looking document that looked suspiciously like a marriage certificate. Alden couldn't suppress his groan. Served him right for doing anything but getting some much-needed sleep after the week he'd had. Looked like jet lag, lack of sleep, and foolish quantities of alcohol made for a treacherous combination in the city of sin.

Hannah followed his gaze, dread flooding her features.

"We have to do something, Alden. This is a horrible mistake."

"Right. Of course," he answered. But all he wanted to do right now was swallow gallons of water and several anti-inflammatory tablets.

"We have to go back to that chapel. See if they can undo…" She lifted a shaky finger, pointing to the signed piece of paper on the ground that he could clearly read now that said *Certificate of Marriage*.

Hannah continued, "Or we have to find a legal office. See about some kind of annulment."

Before Alden could respond, the smartwatch on his wrist dinged with a notification. Absentmindedly, he glanced down at the message, then swore yet again.

"What is it?" Hannah demanded to know. "What else could there possibly be?"

Alden rubbed a palm down his face in frustration. Turned out there was indeed more.

She was married. To Alden Hamid, no less.

So not the way she'd anticipated her nuptials to go. She'd come to this wedding against her better judgment and had somehow gotten hitched before the actual bridal couple had.

How in the world could she have let this happen?

How could either of them not have had the good sense to stop it before the cataclysmic result that had resulted in them now becoming man and wife?

One theory was fairly obvious. She'd always been attracted to Alden. And the man he was now had sent all sorts of hormonal longings that she'd long thought dormant kicking into overdrive.

Stealing another glance at him, it was no wonder. Even under the dire circumstances, it was hard not to stare at the sheer image of male beauty that was Alden. Toned chest and arms.

He wore his boxer briefs like the models on one of those billboards above the buildings in Boston's fashion district.

Enough of that. Those kinds of thoughts were the last thing she needed.

Or another theory might be more plausible. That her wounded feminine pride had been eager to make some kind of recovery after being so unceremoniously dumped.

Maybe all the above. Adding alcohol to that mix had been fuel on the proverbial fire.

Alden's watch pinged again before he'd been able to explain what the first message had been about.

She pointed at his wrist "What's going on?"

He gave her a steady stare, his eyes darkening with sympathy. "Hate to be the bearer of more bad news but we don't really have time to try and unravel this mess at the moment."

Hannah swallowed past the hard lump in her throat. "Why is that?"

"My calendar app and several messages from my best friend, who happens to be the groom, are reminding me that I'm expected at a brunch for close friends and family of the bride and groom. Of course, you would be expected there too."

Hannah groaned out loud. She'd totally forgotten all about the brunch. Heck, she'd pretty much forgotten what day it was. Friday. The wedding was tomorrow. Which meant today was filled with events and get-togethers. Starting with an elaborate brunch for the bridal party and other special guests. "How much time do we have?"

His lips thinned. "Barely more than an hour."

Oh, no. This was a disaster. Every last part of it. "That hardly gives me enough time to shower and brush and throw a decent outfit on."

Hannah sucked in a deep breath. Where was her dress? She couldn't very well traipse through this hotel wearing nothing but her bra and panties.

Oh, God.

She was still cavorting around in her bra and panties. In front of Alden. She had to get dressed ASAP. Then she had to get back to her own room. Now that she was thinking about it, she wasn't even sure where her own room was. This hotel was a massive hotel/casino/convention center.

First things first. Where had she thrown her dress? Or maybe Alden had taken it off her. That thought had heat rushing to her cheeks. She had woken up in his suite, on his mattress, curled up against his side.

All that alluded to a possibility she'd been avoiding speculating on. Had they...?

Hannah gave her head a brisk shake. She couldn't deal with that question just now, as pressing as it was. She simply didn't have the time nor the mental bandwidth.

"I have to find my dress."

He finished throwing on a pair of gray sweatpants and glanced around the room. "It's gotta be here somewhere."

Hannah had to resist the urge to ask him to put a shirt on. Or the temptation to heed that shoulder devil again might be strong enough to have her pulling him back onto the bed.

Luckily, Alden distracted her from that train of thought by locating her dress. It had been hiding in plain sight below the glass coffee table. How had she missed it?

She thanked him and quickly threw it on.

"You're welcome," he answered.

Hannah rammed a hand through her curls, her heart hammering in her chest. Between her physical discomfort and the shock flooding her system, she was sorely tempted to just crawl back into bed and forget any of this was even happening. To be oblivious again to reality, as she'd been just a few minutes earlier. When she'd been snuggled close and warm in Alden's arms.

She bit out a curse under her breath.

"What's that?" Alden asked.

Hannah gave her head a shake. "Nothing. I was just thinking that we absolutely can't mention any of this to Max and Mandy. Or to anyone else, for that matter."

Alden nodded once. "Agreed. This weekend should be all about the two of them."

"Agreed," she repeated, with a nod of her own.

Several moments passed in awkward silence. Finally, Alden cleared his throat. "As far as getting ready goes, I don't have to do much. I'll help you. Whatever you need."

"I might need to take you up on that. Thank you," she said, and meant it with her whole heart. He could probably start with helping her uncover the mystery of exactly where her room was and how she might be able to get into it, considering there was no room key in sight.

He shrugged and smiled at her with a playful wink. For a split second, the sheer beauty that was Alden Hamid served to take her breath away and she could easily see why in an altered, uninhibited state of mind she would have pledged to marry him with eager enthusiasm.

"You're welcome," he answered. "It's what any decent husband would do."

Too soon. He really shouldn't have said what he had about being her husband. Alden cringed inwardly as he glanced about the banquet hall where the brunch was to be held. Not like the word meant anything in this case. They weren't really married. That certificate was nothing more than a piece of paper obtained during a drunken, reckless night when their nostalgia for the past had overcome their good sense. It never would have happened if he'd been his usual disciplined self. If he'd gotten any kind of sleep over the past two days.

No wonder Hannah's eyes had widened and she'd somehow gone a shade paler as the word had left his mouth.

He scanned the room once more. No sign of her still. Not surprising. By the time they'd located her purse—somehow it had ended up behind the heavy curtain in the main sitting room of his suite—and hence her key card, then made their way to her room on the other side of the hotel, she barely had half an hour to get ready.

Maybe he should go check on her. But before the thought had fully formed in his brain, he watched as she rushed in through the double doors of the main entrance.

His breath caught when he saw her. The woman sure could clean up well. And she'd done so in an impressively short amount of time.

Even from where he stood at a distance across

the hall, she was downright striking. She wore some kind of flowing, breezy, silky number in navy that brought out the amber highlights in her dark hair, which was done up atop her crown with a few tendrils escaping along the sides of her face. Her face looked fresh and flushed, and gone were the streaks of dark mascara from this morning. As if the messy morning they'd awoken to had never even happened.

His wife.

The word popped into his head without warning. He dismissed it with haste. He had no real right to call her that. There was no meaning behind it in their case. Again, he hadn't been himself last night. He was bitter and tired and angry about this damn deal that was causing him much more of a headache than anticipated. And Hannah had gotten caught up in his mess.

He really should apologize. He should do it now.

She was still scrambling around, trying to figure out where to sit. He began making his way over to her but didn't get very far. A noisy ruckus erupted from the settee area. The sound of a microphone being turned on rang through the air before a loud voice began speaking.

"If everyone could take their seats, the bride and groom have arrived."

Alden glanced down at the place card he'd picked up at the doorway with his name on it. Table number thirteen. Not his lucky number, it turned out. Because he happened to be standing next to table eleven. And he could see Hannah pulling out a chair across the room. Or rather, a tall gentleman with a wide smile wearing a tan shirt was pulling it out for her. A wave of frustration surged through him when the same man pulled out the chair next to her and sat down.

"Alden, it looks like you're sitting here next to me," a soft feminine voice sounded behind him.

He didn't have to turn around to recognize the owner. Alyssa Cambell. That confirmed it. Nope. Luck definitely was not on his side at the moment.

With a resigned sigh, he forced a smile on his face and turned toward his assigned table. Alyssa patted the seat of the chair next to her as he pulled it out.

"I'm glad it worked out this way," she said as soon as he sat down. "We didn't get a chance to chat at all yesterday before we were interrupted." The last word dripped with disdain.

Alyssa had no idea how grateful he'd been for that interruption at the time. Nor how much he wished for the same respite to come his way right at the moment. He stole a glance at the source of that interruption. Hannah had her head back, her hand to her throat in the middle of a hearty laugh. Whatever tall tan-shirt dude had just told her had apparently been hilarious.

Alden felt the muscles around his stomach clench tight. It should be him sitting there next to her. Alden should be the one making her laugh so delightfully with such abandon. He was her hus— He cut off the thought before he could complete it.

"Is everything all right?" he heard Alyssa ask next to him and forced his eyes back on her.

"Of course. Everything's great. Why do you ask?"

"Because you look like you just saw someone steal your car or something." She clasped at her chest with fingers spread. "I had that happen to me last year, you know. What. A. Nightmare."

What the devil was she talking about?

Alden listened with half an ear as she recounted the ordeal of the time she left the Lucky Lady boutique last year only to find her Mercedes gone. With her arms full of shopping bags, no less.

"I got divorced last year, you know," Alyssa suddenly declared. No longer skirting around the subject apparently.

Ironic. He'd just gotten married last night.

"What's so funny?" Alyssa asked.

Damn it. He hadn't realized he'd actually laughed out loud.

"Oh, nothing," he quickly told her. "Just wondering where the food is."

That was true enough. To add to his other mistakes last night, he couldn't recall taking the time to eat anything. Hannah had to be ravenous too.

Enough.

He had to stop thinking about her. Hannah Devine was out of his league. She always had been. That's why he'd never worked up the courage to ask her out back in high school. Hannah was furiously smart, raised by a single mother who would have done anything for her. Unlike Alden who'd grown up in a broken family that had eventually completely shattered. Hannah deserved the kind of loyalty and stability she'd grown up with. Alden knew he wasn't the kind of man who could give her those things in life.

The sooner they got this sham of a marriage dissolved, the better. His mind was just messing with him. Taunting him that the girl he'd gone to high school with, who'd accompanied him to various school events simply because they'd been friends with two other people who were a couple, had just happened to become his wife last night.

Well, he'd have to fix that. As soon as this brunch was over, he'd go get Hannah and they'd find the nearest legal office.

Then it would all be over.

CHAPTER THREE

THE MORE SHE sobered up, the more horrified Hannah felt.

To think, she was sitting here, trying to make small talk with this stranger when she'd gotten married to Alden last night.

She was doing her best to pay attention to what the man seated next to her was saying, he was certainly a talker. Hannah was making sure to laugh at all the appropriate times, nod when it seemed needed. But it wasn't easy. She couldn't seem to shake thoughts of Alden or what had happened between them last night.

In her haste to get ready and make it to brunch on time, she'd almost forgotten to take the wedding ring off. Now she was hyperaware of it sitting in a small pocket of her clutch purse. It had to have cost a pretty penny. What if she lost it? She had to remember to give it back to Alden at the soonest possible moment.

What lousy timing this brunch was. She and

Alden desperately needed to talk. Even more importantly, they needed to see about fixing the mess they were both in. Instead, she was sitting here listening to one of Max's golf buddies droning on and on about the importance of investing in a high-quality putter.

Where was Alden, anyway?

Why hadn't he so much as tried to contact her since they'd left each other earlier? Granted, it hadn't been that long ago. But one would think... Actually, she didn't know what to think. What was the proper protocol when you woke up married to someone you hadn't even seen in person since high school?

She had no right to judge him.

That gracious feeling fled when she finally spotted him across the room. Next to Alyssa Cambell, who was sitting fully turned in his direction, her palm resting on his forearm. A spike of annoyance shot through her chest, one she refused to acknowledge as some sort of jealousy.

Because that would make no sense. It wasn't like Alden was really her husband. Well, on paper he was, but only legally. Which sounded ridiculous when one thought about it.

She stole another glance in his direction. He appeared to be hanging on Alyssa's every word. He had a dark suit jacket hung on the back of his chair. The deep burgundy-colored shirt he wore fit him like a glove, unbuttoned at the collar with the sleeves rolled down midway to his elbows. Even from here, she could see the toned, muscular definition of his shoulders and arms. Or maybe she was just remembering. After all, those arms had been around her all night. A muscle jumped somewhere in the vicinity of her chest.

And that was enough of that kind of thought.

Her irritation only grew with each course. By the time dessert was served Hannah had to remind herself to unclench her jaw. Every time she looked up, Alyssa's chair had somehow gotten even closer to Alden's. The woman was going to end up on his lap at this rate.

She stabbed at the chocolate cake that a server set in front of her and shoved a full forkful in her mouth.

"Like chocolate, huh?" the golfer asked. What was his name? Brett? Brad? She hadn't really been paying attention. How could Alden be enjoying himself? Had he forgotten their foolish circumstances? He should be stressing the same way she was.

Brett/Brad interrupted her thoughts. "Would you like mine?" he asked, pushing his plate of cake over to her on the table.

Hannah glanced down to realize with some

surprise that she'd devoured her entire dessert. More the pity, she couldn't recall even tasting it. She could blame Alden for that too. He'd ruined her enjoyment of a perfectly good confection. It was at that moment she looked his way again only to find him staring right back at her. Was it her imagination or did he look equally as perturbed as she felt?

Brett/Brad began to speak again. "So, you went to school with Max and Mandy?"

"That's right," she answered absentmindedly, not tearing her gaze away from Alden's. He finally looked away first when Alyssa pulled her phone up to show him something on the screen.

With the meal finally over, Hannah pushed back her chair. "Guess it's time to mingle," she told Brett/Brad with a wide smile. "It was nice to meet you," she added, then stood and bolted before she learned any more about golf.

"Yeah, you too," he replied after a startled pause, but Hannah was already walking away. He'd seemed nice enough. But she had enough on her hands thanks to those of the male persuasion. Between the almost fiancé who'd dumped her, and the guy she'd ended up hitched to, her proverbial plate was full. The last thing she needed was to entertain some kind of flirtation with yet a third.

That little devil from before reappeared on

her shoulder. The little cretin had the nerve to laugh at her! Right. That's why you're rushing off to Alden's side.

As annoying as it was, the words gave her pause. She couldn't very well interrupt Alyssa and Alden's conversation yet again. Once could be overlooked. If Hannah did it again, it might look like the start of a pattern. Alyssa was the type to call her on it too. How would she answer? It wasn't as if she could explain that she needed Alden to accompany her to their quickie divorce.

So now she was standing in the middle of the banquet hall just hovering. The ladies' room. She could go freshen up and buy herself some time. Hopefully, Alden would have extricated himself from Alyssa's possessive grip by the time she was done. And she could certainly use a little freshening.

When she stepped out of the ladies' lounge moments later, Alden was waiting for her in the hallway.

"Here." He extended a sweaty glass in her direction. "I brought you this."

Hannah immediately shook her head. "Did you really bring me a drink?"

"It's just mineral water. Figured you could still use the hydrating. I sure as hell do."

"In that case, thank you." She took the offering and indulged in several deep gulps. Alden was right. After their bingeing last night, Hannah didn't think she'd ever feel quenched again in her lifetime.

She wiped her mouth with the back of her hand. "Are you ready to get out of here and take care of what we need to take care of?"

He stepped to the side and motioned for her to lead the way. "After you."

They didn't get far before they were stopped in their tracks.

"I've been looking everywhere for you!" Mandy seemed to appear out of nowhere in front of them to pull Hannah by the shoulders into a tight bear hug. When she finally let go, she poked Alden in the chest with a manicured finger. "And Max keeps asking where you might be."

Max materialized then as unexpectedly as his wife-to-be had a moment ago. What kind of couple's sorcery was this? His and Hannah's path out of the banquet hall had seemed clear only a moment ago. Or maybe they'd just been distracted.

"I sure have," Max agreed. "You've been AWOL, bro," he said, cuffing Alden on the shoulder.

Mandy's eyes narrowed as she looked from

Alden to Hannah, then back and forth once more. "And now we find you here together. Imagine that," she added, suspicion laced in her voice.

Her groom nodded along in agreement.

"You left the party last night before we got a chance to talk. You both did."

Hannah clasped her hands in front of her chest. "I'm really sorry about that, Mandy. I was just so tired after flying out here. And besides, you looked pretty busy with the other guests. I didn't want to add to the frenzy."

"Hmm," was all Mandy replied with, before adding, "Well, here you both are finally. Together." She emphasized the last word again, another flash of suspicion behind her eyes.

She was onto them.

"We were catching up," Alden supplied. "I haven't seen Hannah in a while. And we were about to come find you."

That was a lie.

It dawned on Alden how remiss he and Hannah had been. Of course, Max and Mandy would miss them. Between the party last night and rushing out of the banquet today, that type of behavior would be certain to raise a fair amount of curiosity from their hosts. In Alden and Hannah's defense, they'd had some pressing matters to contend with and other things on their minds.

Mandy grasped Hannah by the hand. "Well, now that you two have caught up with each other, it's our turn."

Hannah's smile faltered. "Of course. I'd love that. I know I've said it before, but I'm so happy for the two of you."

"Thanks, Hannah," Mandy said, then punched her groom on the arm playfully. "Took long enough for this big lug to finally propose."

Max shrugged. "Just trying to preserve my bachelor days a little longer. We can't all be players with the ladies like my Alden here."

Was it his imagination or did Hannah let out an almost silent huff at those words? Wishful thinking, most likely. Though why he would wish such a thing made no sense.

Mandy stepped closer to Hannah, laid her hand on her arm. "I heard about your breakup. How are you doin', hon?"

Hannah's mouth tightened. "Fine. I'm just fine."

Mandy gave Hannah's arm a motherly pat. "Forget about that idiot. He doesn't know what he had and gave up."

Alden's thoughts echoed with a muffled memory of him uttering those very same words to

Hannah sometime last night. Right before he proved them to her by proposing to her himself.

Mandy continued, "Your time to walk down the aisle is right around the corner too, Hannah. I just know it."

Alden could feel Hannah's slight cringe next to him while he groaned inwardly. If Max and Mandy only knew.

"Thanks, Mandy," Hannah replied with a gracious smile. "But I really am doing fine. And Justin and I are officially over. For good," she added with emphasis.

The rush of satisfaction Alden felt at those words shouldn't have been as strong as it was.

Mandy pulled Hannah closer. "What you need is a day of pampering. My sisters and I have full massages and facials scheduled in about half an hour."

Mandy's bridesmaids were her three sisters. As Max's groomsmen were his three brothers.

"You absolutely have to join us, Hannah," Mandy said.

Hannah immediately began to argue but she was promptly shut down. "I won't take no for an answer."

Hannah glanced at Alden, her eyes wild. If she was looking for a solution from his direction, he didn't have one for her. "Um—"

Mandy cut her off again. "Look, if you're

worried about imposing, that makes no sense. You know I would have included you in the bridal party if Max and I hadn't decided to go with a small one with family only."

"Oh, that's not…" Hannah trailed off.

"Same goes for me, bro," Max added. "You'd have absolutely been one of the groomsmen. Without question."

Alden knew the truth of that without a doubt. He'd harbored no hard feelings about not being included in the bridal party. He understood. Not that he knew from personal experience, but he imagined weddings were hard enough to plan without worrying about offending friends. So many major and minor decisions to make. Unless, of course, the couple eloped in a drunken and sleepless stupor after gambling the night away.

"Their spa excursion works for us too, bud," Max was saying.

"Yeah?"

Max nodded. "My brothers and I have a full eighteen-hole round of golf scheduled. But Tom's gout is acting up. All these fancy buffets aren't helping. You can round out the fourth spot."

Alden cast what he hoped was an imperceptible glance at Hannah. Her eyes conveyed a clear message that said, *What choice do we have?*

She was right. They really didn't have a choice. Turning either offer down wasn't an option. They couldn't very well explain why they had alternate plans for the rest of the day. Not without admitting they'd gotten married. To each other.

"Sounds great," Alden answered the other man with resignation. "Give me a chance to change and I'll meet you in the lobby."

Looked like their divorce or annulment—he wasn't even sure what applied in their circumstance—whichever it was, was going to have to wait.

There was salad on her face.

Hannah twitched her nose and maneuvered her cheek muscles until the slices of cucumbers on her eyes fell back into place after slipping when she'd just sneezed. The seaweed wrapped along her jawline up to her forehead smelled of ocean and lime.

She, along with Mandy, had opted for the facial first while her friend's three sisters had gone with the massage as their first choice.

Now lying side by side in lounge chairs, Hannah was doing all she could to pay attention to the conversation at hand. She hoped her friend wasn't noticing just how distracted she was. In her defense, this was the first time she'd woken up as a married woman, then had to rush out to yet another wedding.

Mandy's next words pulled her right out of her distraction. "So, you and Alden seemed to be spending a lot of time together last night."

Hannah couldn't be sure how the other woman might have known that, so figured it was a lucky guess on her part.

"Just catching up," she answered, which was true enough.

"And you're both here solo," Mandy said, stating the obvious.

Hannah knew where her friend was going with this. She refused to take the bait. "I'm looking forward to the massage," she said, an attempt to change the subject. It didn't work.

"You know, we always thought you two would somehow end up together," Mandy said.

There it was. It hadn't taken her friend long at all to just come out and say it.

"Nothing in common," Hannah answered. "Not then. And not now."

"Hmm," was Mandy's only response.

Hannah sucked in a breath around her avocado face mask. "Why would you ever think we might have ended up together? He never even so much as asked me out. While he'd asked out half the female student body by year three."

Hannah wanted to kick herself for the way

her voice hitched as the words left her mouth. As if she were disappointed or somehow miserable about the truth of her statement. As if she'd been waiting all those years ago for Alden to ask her and he never had.

That was so not what she'd meant.

In an attempt to try and recover, she quickly added, "Which was just as well. Like I said, nothing in common."

Mandy was silent for several moments. When she finally replied, it was just with another, "Hmm."

Only this time, it sounded much more knowing.

Where was Alden?

Hannah dropped her gaze back down to her smartwatch without actually noticing the time. She already knew it couldn't be more than a minute or so past the last time she'd looked when it was after 10:00 p.m.

Much too late to try and amend their mistake of the previous night now. No legal offices were open this late. Not even in Vegas. No. The only establishments still open at this hour were the casinos, shows, and those cursed chapels like the one she and Alden had frequented last night. Or early this morning, to be more accurate. Chapels for the impulsive and reckless couples who wanted to get married without giving it too much thought.

Hannah sighed. She supposed most of those couples were genuinely in love when they made their vows in front of Elvis. Like the man and woman they'd encountered last night. Whereas she and Alden had just been drunk and foolish and swimming in memories.

Love had nothing to do with it in their case. Hannah gave herself a mental thwack. What was she even doing? Entertaining thoughts about love where Alden was concerned? Sure, she'd been attracted to him since they were kids. Had often thought about him over the years. In her more unguarded moments, she'd sometimes caught herself comparing the memories of him with the man she'd thought she'd end up legitimately marrying.

Thoughts of Justin only served to sour her mood further so she pushed them aside. Right now, the only thing she needed to focus on was getting ahold of Alden so that they could work on a plan B regarding rectifying their careless mistake of a marriage.

She texted him once more and received a response only moments later. Yet another version of the same replies he'd been sending all evening.

Can't break away just yet. Have tried. Will explain when I see you.

Hannah cursed and paced around her room. Compared to Alden's suite, her own lodgings would be considered postage-stamp-sized.

This was pointless. Surely, they weren't going to solve anything tonight. She may as well just go to bed. She'd already brushed her teeth and scrubbed her face, still tingling from the hour-long facial Mandy had so generously treated her to this afternoon before a ninety-minute massage. As inconvenient as the timing was, the pampering had indeed done her a world of good and wonders toward soothing her nerves. But now she felt tense and frazzled yet again.

She'd begun to pull the covers back to crawl under them when her phone tinged with a message. Alden.

On my way to hotel now. Can we talk? I think we need to.

Hannah grunted out a frustrated laugh. Oh, so now he wanted to talk finally, did he? Now that the time was so late. While she'd been here pacing for hours, trying to come up with a solution to their predicament. Well, damned if she was going to get dressed and rush to meet him somewhere.

She responded right away.

Already in my pj's. Please come up here to my room.

The least he could do was come to her. After all the waiting she'd been doing for him.

The response was immediate.

Will do. See you soon.

Hannah resumed her pacing. A frizzle of electricity ran over her skin. She didn't know the cause but was absolutely certain that it had nothing to do with the anticipation or excitement about seeing Alden in the next few minutes.

She had not been missing him all day. Absolutely not. And the way that Mandy had gushed throughout the afternoon about being so in love had most certainly not led to any kind of longing within her heart. Nor had all of Mandy's words about how she'd thought that Alden and Hannah would eventually get together back in school.

No. None of it was material to her current mood. She was just hurting after the unexpected rejection by Justin she hadn't seen coming. Those feelings of longing had nothing to do with Alden himself.

The lady doth protest too much...

She pushed the silly quote away. In fact, she was more than annoyed with Alden at the moment. How could he have not found some way to get back to the resort earlier so that they could do something about this mess? And now that it was too late in the day, he was finally making his way back and asking to see her.

By the time she heard the knock on the door, her annoyance had grown to ire. She yanked the door open so fast and hard, the hinge made a swishing noise. He looked her up and down with an amused smile when she stepped aside to let him in.

"Nice sleepwear."

Hannah glanced down at the only set of pj's she'd packed—a loose tank and matching boy shorts adorned with penguins on a ski slope wearing long scarves and colorful hats. She'd been a bit preoccupied packing only her suitcase. Justin had often asked her to pack for him too whenever they traveled together, following a detailed list of all the items he required.

Her ire grew at the thought of all the ways she'd indulged the man only to end up here at a wedding, single. Except, technically, she wasn't.

Alden pointed toward the vicinity of her chest. "What's that particular penguin doing?"

She was in no mood. "Skiing. They're all skiing, Alden."

"Cute," he said, stepping farther into the room.

She followed close behind. "Never mind my attire, why in the world did you take so long to get back here?"

He raised an eyebrow. "I told you. I couldn't."

"Really? You've been gone for hours. Eighteen holes does not take that long."

He crossed his arms in front of his chest, and the amused grin had grown wider, which only served to grow her irritation even further. She couldn't even be sure who she was more sore with at the moment—Alden or Justin.

"What's so funny?"

He leaned over to tap her on the nose. "Are you really irate with me about golfing with the boys? It's like we really are married."

She gave him a useless shove. "Ha, ha. Very funny. You know very well it's not out of some kind of wifely concern."

But then his smile suddenly faded and his brows drew together. Hannah studied his face; far from appearing relaxed and recharged after a leisurely day of golf, Alden could be described as the complete opposite. He looked weary and haggard. His hair was matted in the outline of a sports cap, as if he'd just recently taken it off. Which made no sense. They couldn't have been on the course all this time. "There's a reason I didn't rush back," he said, his voice gravelly rough.

His serious expression tempered her annoyance. Something was not right.

"What's that? Is something wrong?"

He nodded. "In fact there is. Seriously wrong. We have a bit of a situation."

CHAPTER FOUR

HANNAH WASN'T QUITE ready to breathe a sigh of relief when she made her way to the pew and took a seat. Might be too early to celebrate just yet. In fact, she was still shaking inside, ever since hearing what Alden had told her last night—Max had been getting cold feet. After sending away the other men after golfing, he'd apparently confided to his friend what he hadn't been able to tell his brothers.

Max was inches close to calling the whole thing off. And he'd told Alden this with less than twelve hours before the wedding.

That would have been a catastrophe. Poor Mandy would have been devastated to say the least. So Alden had spent the rest of the evening talking him down, trying to reassure him that it was just pre-wedding jitters until he'd convinced him finally.

Hannah hadn't seen Alden at all today either. He was making sure to stick by Max's side to ensure the groom's feet stayed warm. Which meant they still hadn't done anything about ending their own marriage. Yet again. It was almost as if there was some strange force in the universe preventing her and Alden from undoing what they'd so carelessly done.

But Hannah couldn't worry about any of that now. All that mattered at the moment was that Max went through with his nuptials. Surely, he wouldn't back out now, at ground zero? Most of the guests had assembled. The altar was all set up, the flowers arranged.

Though not quite a full breath, she breathed a sigh of relief when Alden appeared at the doorway, then made his way over to sit next to her. It had to be a good sign that he was here.

"Well?" she whispered, leaning slightly toward him. The smell of his new upscale aftershave tickled her nose and it occurred to her that she'd already grown familiar with its scent. With Alden's scent. She used that familiarity now to let it soothe her. As did Alden's mere presence. She hadn't realized just how on edge she'd been since hearing about Max's ambivalence last night.

Alden took her hand and gave it a reassuring squeeze. "Crisis averted."

Hannah finally released the remainder of the breath she'd been holding. "Phew. I mean, I thought you must have convinced him to see reason but I didn't want to assume."

Alden didn't let go of her hand. She made no attempt to remove it. "I admit, it was touch and go for much too long there for a while. Long enough to shave some years off my life."

"Thank heavens it's a go," she answered. Still, she wouldn't be able to totally relax until the vows were said and done. That was way too close. Damn Max for even considering walking away. And heaven help him if he left Mandy at the altar. Aside from an angry mob, which included Mandy's parents, sisters, and cousins, he would have Hannah herself to contend with.

"I just don't know what he was thinking," Hannah said, still making sure to keep her voice down. "He and Mandy belong together. They've known each other for decades."

Alden's response was to merely squeeze her hand once more. After an eternity, which realistically could have only been a few minutes, the organ player finally appeared and began to play. Right on cue, a dark-haired little moppet of a toddler skipped down the aisle, dropping rose petals in her wake. Hannah recognized her as the youngest of Mandy's three nieces. She was followed by her soon-to-be uncles, Max's brothers. They lined up next to the altar.

The bridesmaids walked down next to take

their place on the other side of the altar. After several seconds of delay that left everyone craning their necks toward the entrance, a very distracted little boy in a pint-sized tuxedo appeared, holding a satin pillow. He took his time walking down the aisle, eliciting chuckles from the attendees. Finally, Max appeared and Hannah's heart skipped in her chest at the sight of him. Pale and hesitant, he looked like he wanted to dash in the opposite direction.

"Don't you dare," she heard Alden utter under his breath. He looked for all purposes like a man ready to jump into action if needed, though for the life of her, Hannah wouldn't be able to guess what he might possibly do to avert such a disaster. Still, the fact that he was so ready to intervene had something quivering in the pit of her stomach. Alden cared for his friends. Deeply.

Too bad he'd never given any kind of indication that he cared for her the same way. He'd written her down as his backup option junior year. The thought had floored her the other night when he'd told her. She still found it hard to believe. Still. It meant nothing. It was a silly little exercise that no one had taken seriously. Except for her.

Finally, Max made his way down to stand next to his brothers.

The organ music changed to the traditional "Wedding March" and a collective intake of breath sounded throughout the chapel as Mandy appeared on her father's arm.

The look on Max's face as the pair made their way down the aisle toward him said it all—they'd really had nothing to worry about. Pure, intense love shone from every feature of the man's face. He really had been mistaking his pre-wedding jitters for second thoughts. Thank heavens he'd been made to come to his senses. Thanks to Alden.

Alden had been so right to make sure his friend hadn't made a mistake he might never have recovered from.

She felt the now familiar and reassuring tightness around her palm and looked down to find that not only was her hand still gripped tightly in Alden's, he'd tucked it into the crook of his arm. She hadn't noticed the movement because it had felt so natural.

Hannah couldn't help the direction her imagination took her in. How would it feel to be walked down the aisle as the man you wanted to spend the rest of your life with awaited you? Images formed in her mind's eye. In them, she wore a dress similar to the one Mandy wore now, but the tail was longer, the neckline more V-shaped. The bouquet she held was made up of red and pink roses rather than the lilies Mandy carried.

Her breath hitched as the pictures in her mind's eye rounded out. The man waiting at the altar for her wasn't Justin.

It was Alden.

His luck appeared to be better this time around. Alden reached for his name card for the dinner and reception, relieved to see that his and Hannah's both read the same table number, unlike at the brunch yesterday.

Hopefully, Alyssa would be sitting at an entirely different one. He had nothing against the woman; he just wanted to relax a bit now that the stress of the past twenty-four hours was finally behind him. Max and Mandy were safely married. He'd be able to enjoy this dinner and finally focus on Hannah and Hannah alone.

He knew very well she was eager to discuss how to end their marriage union officially once and for all. Maybe if they got some time alone, they'd be able to discuss how, at last.

Except...if he were being honest with himself, he had to admit to a bit of ambivalence about the whole thing. At some point, the idea of being married to Hannah had somehow become more and more feasible, not such a ridiculous notion. Less of an error in need of an urgent remedy.

Which made absolutely no sense. Of course, they couldn't just stay married.

Could they?

Alden gave his head a brisk shake and made his way to the assigned table. Hannah hadn't made it into the ballroom yet. Like so many other inexplicable things about the way he felt about her, he seemed to be able to instinctively tell when she was nearby.

He couldn't even be sure when the idea to maybe put off the divorce had wound its way into his head. At some point during yesterday and today, while with Max, he'd found some of the advice he was doling out to his friend about marriage was also resonating with himself as well. Advice such as what good fortune it was to be tied to someone you'd always cared for. How lucky he was to have found a woman like Mandy—talented, lovely both inside and out, accomplished.

All those traits could be attributed to Hannah. And many more.

The moment he'd laid eyes on her again at the rooftop cabana, he'd felt a jolt of an emotion he couldn't really place. Familiarity mixed with something else, something much more heated. All the ways he'd felt attracted to her when they were younger came flooding back to wash over him. He'd tried to tell himself that what he'd felt back then was nothing more than teenage hormonal longing. That argument held much less weight now that they were both adults.

Was it that ridiculous a notion that the two of them might end up together? The way they'd each written on that silly, adolescent question-naire? Maybe his inebriated and sleep-deprived subconscious knew what it was doing when it helped him into that chapel the other night.

Maybe Hannah's had done the same.

Sure, their marriage had come about in a wholly untraditional and unplanned way, but some things happened for a reason. He knew that firsthand.

Look at where his life had led to after one impulsive decision to walk into the lobby of the Reardon hotel when he was sixteen to ask for a job. Fifteen years, a lot of hard work, blood and sweat later, he was a name to be reckoned with in the hospitality industry. That sixteen-year-old kid would have never guessed.

As far as he and Hannah were concerned, the timing was almost uncanny. They were both at a crossroads, Hannah having just left a rela-tionship while he was on the verge of a major business expansion in which it would only be beneficial and work in his favor to be a married man.

Just as he knew he would, he sensed the moment Hannah arrived. Spotting him, she made a beeline directly for him as she flashed him a wide smile, the sight of which did quirky things to his gut. He stood and pulled out a chair for her next to him.

"Looks like you saved the day," she said, taking her seat. "Well done, Mr. Hamid."

"Thank you, Mrs. Hamid." The words slipped out of his mouth before he'd had a chance to catch them. Now there was no taking them back.

Whoa.

Hadn't he sworn back in the hotel room that first morning that he'd be more careful with his words when it came to their fake slash real marriage?

"Uh...sorry," he said immediately, registering the instant look of shock on Hannah's face. Yeah, well, he'd shocked himself too. He could hardly blame her for her reaction at his slip. This was why he had to be so careful entertaining thoughts like the ones he'd had earlier. He was on a slippery slope that would only take Hannah down with him if he lost his footing.

Speaking of apologies. It was about time he made one for his real transgression.

"Look, what happened the other night, the way I got drunk and where we ended up. I hadn't slept in two days because of a complicated business meeting overseas. Then I flew straight here. It was irresponsible of me to have so many drinks given how tired and sleepless I was. I know it's no excuse—" What a word salad. God. He was making a mess of this.

Hannah sat, blinking at him.

"I just wanted to say I'm sorry for all of it."

She nodded once, then reached for her water. Swallowed several gulps before turning back to him to answer. "I'm just as much to blame for what happened that night, Alden. I'm not some helpless nitwit who simply followed a man into a chapel."

"That's not what I'm implying."

She held a hand up. "I could give you a litany of reasons why I let my guard down so completely also. But those reasons would be excuses too. The fact remains that it happened. And there's nothing we can do about it tonight. Or tomorrow for that matter, given that it's Sunday. So we may as well enjoy this meal and this reception. And deal with our own mess at the first opportunity."

He held his own glass out to her in a mock salute. "Wise words. That works for me."

She suddenly looked away, as if unable to

continue holding his gaze. "I do have one question, however." Her cheeks were growing redder by the moment. "We haven't really had a chance to discuss it. And I'm horrified that I have to ask."

He immediately knew what she was referring to. She wanted to know if they'd consummated the marriage.

He quickly shook his head, completely certain of the answer. *That* had not happened between them. He had no doubt. For he was certain that every cell in his body would be aware of having made love with Hannah. She wasn't the type of woman a man might forget touching, holding, being intimate with. The blood rushed away from his extremities and he had to rein himself in to focus on the conversation at hand.

"No, we fell asleep as soon as we hit the mattress and stayed that way."

Clasping a hand to her chest, Hannah blew out a loud breath in relief, then clinked her glass to his still upheld one. "To Max and Mandy."

"To Max and Mandy," he repeated.

He had to stop saying such things to her. Didn't he know what it did to her insides when he referred to her as his wife? Alden might be taking this whole marriage thing lightly, but in the couple short days they'd become man and wife—on paper—Hannah found her confused head often blurring the lines between what was real and what wasn't.

Max had called Alden a player and a ladies' man. He had such a reputation for a reason. It was hardly any wonder all of this meant so little to him.

Still, illogical though it may be, it was hard not to compare Alden to the other men in this room. Or to other men in general. Successful, handsome, driven, considerate. The way he filled out a tux could make a nun swoon. Alden would be considered any girl's dream catch. If he ever actually wanted to be caught. All indications said otherwise.

What might it be like to really be married to him? In all manner of ways?

Stop it.

The surroundings were just getting to her, that's all. Given how lovely Mandy and Max's ceremony had been, then the atmosphere in this ballroom, one could hardly blame a girl for entertaining fanciful thoughts about her own romantic future.

"Here they are," Alden said, pulling her out of her thoughts. Mandy and Max had entered the ballroom and were making their way over to the dance floor. A raucous round of applause followed by a standing ovation greeted them as they began their first dance together as man and wife. Mandy's smile had enough wattage to light up a large city. None the worse for wear. Thankfully, she seemed to have no knowledge of how close this magical moment had come to not even happening.

The evening could have been much less celebratory and bordering more on tragic.

"I'm so glad Max came to his senses," she said in Alden's ear, low enough that their fellow tablemates wouldn't be able to hear over the music. "They both look so happy."

"Thank goodness she has no idea."

"I hope she never finds out." Hannah didn't want to think about what that might do to their relationship or the start of their married life together. "She's radiant, isn't she?"

Alden nodded his agreement but his gaze was fixated on her rather than on the couple on the dance floor. "Absolutely beautiful."

Hannah's breath caught, her heart doing somersaults in her chest. His words were spoken directly at her, his eyes fixed on her face.

He finally looked away, not that it did anything to break the heavy tension between them. "I mean your dress," he said, gesturing toward her. "It's very original. I meant to compliment you on the one you wore yesterday also. Very unique designs."

Hannah glanced down at the jade-colored dress she wore, rimmed at the bottom with delicate black lace.

"Thank you. Both dresses are indeed one of a kind, in fact."

He released a low whistle. "Must have cost a good amount in that case. Not that I know much about ladies' fashion. Or anything at all about it really."

She chuckled. "They hardly cost anything."

He raised a surprised eyebrow. "They don't look second-hand."

The turn in conversation made her realize just how little they knew about each other. "The dresses were inexpensive because I made them both myself. I like to design and sew a lot of the clothes I wear."

His eyebrow lifted another millimeter. "Wow. That's really impressive. I would have never guessed."

Why would he? They hadn't exactly kept in touch through the years. She had no idea what Alden's hobbies or interests might be, or if he even had any.

It surprised her to realize that she'd be really interested to learn.

"A corporate accountant who makes her own wardrobe in her spare time."

"Some weeks, my hobby is the only thing that makes the accounting part bearable." Hannah couldn't even be sure why she'd admitted such a thing. She'd never spoken the words out loud before, not to anyone. Not even her mother. Well, especially not to her mother.

Alden's eyes narrowed on her. "You don't like what you do for a living?"

Such a complicated question, she couldn't guess how to begin to answer it. "It's my career. That's all. I don't exactly look forward to Monday mornings if that's any kind of answer."

She'd be looking even less forward to them now. Having to see Justin every weekday. Watching him go about his work, having to confer with him on mutual projects. So that's why everyone advised against becoming romantically involved with a coworker. She should have heeded the advice.

Alden's eyes narrowed on her face. "Maybe you should do something about that."

She shrugged. "A hobby doesn't pay a girl's bills."

"Maybe it could, under the right circumstances. And with the right kind of backing."

Before she could ask him what he might mean by that, the servers appeared with the first course. The food was delicious, and after a crisp and fresh Caesar salad, the main entrée arrived. She'd decided on the grilled salmon with citrus glaze and a side of root vegetables. Alden had gone with the braised beef with buttery mashed potatoes. He scooped a spoonful and deposited it on her side plate without asking.

A memory surfaced in her mind, the way he would share his French fries with her whenever the four of them stopped for fast food after their football games back in high school. He'd done that without so much as a word back then too.

She hadn't given the gesture much thought. Just assumed he wasn't much of a French fry aficionado. So why was she so touched right now that he'd done the same thing all these years later? She shouldn't be.

Most of the meal was spent making small talk with their table neighbors in between bites of food.

Soon the plates were cleared and the band fired up the music once more. Max and Mandy appeared on the dance floor again, motioning for their guests to join them.

Alden gave her a wink and stood. He extended out his hand. "It's only polite to do as the bridal couple ask and dance with them. Shall we?"

Why not? She'd eaten her entire meal and could move around a bit. Plus, it might help release some of the strange tension she'd been feeling ever since her wayward imagination at the chapel earlier.

CHAPTER FIVE

IT DIDN'T SURPRISE her that Alden was a good dancer. The man seemed to be gifted at everything he did. He moved smoothly, not even a hint of awkward stiffness. And he stayed matched to the beat. When the band began playing a song for a group led dance, he knew all the moves and executed them perfectly. Unlike Hannah, who tripped up at least twice, laughing at her clumsiness, especially compared to Alden's dancing skills.

"I must have two left feet," she told him over the notes of the upbeat song. What a cliché.

In response, Alden crossed his own feet at the ankles and did a full circle, ending with a low bow in front of her. Hannah laughed at the perfectly executed move. "Show off."

"Who? Me?" Alden asked with mock outrage.

She was really enjoying herself. When was the last time she'd gone dancing? Not since she'd begun dating Justin. During her college days and years as a new adult professional, she'd gone clubbing with friends as often as she could, to some of Boston's hottest spots. Now, she wouldn't even be able to name one. Most of those friends had moved away in pursuit of their dreams. Justin had declared that dancing just wasn't his thing on one of their first dates when she'd suggested it as an option.

What were the odds she'd be having this much fun if Justin had accompanied her to this wedding? And what did that question say about the future she'd almost embarked on with him?

"Penny for your thoughts," Alden said, leaning closer and raising his voice above the loud music.

She chuckled before answering. "I was just thinking that you appear to be a man of many talents."

"Says the woman who designs and makes her own clothes."

As much as she appreciated the compliment, Hannah didn't really see her craft as any kind of talent. More so a labor of love. Sure, she'd thought about pursuing fashion arts all those years ago when she'd been a naive kid with a world of possibilities ahead of her. That was before her mother had convinced her pursuing a more practical field would make more sense. Her mother was nothing if not practical. And she'd always had very clear ideas about Hannah's pursuits in life.

She could hardly blame Mama. When they'd barely scraped by paycheck to paycheck with Mama's modest earnings as an aide in a care home, it was no wonder her mother had wanted her to pursue a job that provided a more guaranteed income. It wasn't as if her father was around to help. He'd abandoned them so long ago Hannah didn't remember his face any longer.

The last song wrapped up and the soloist tapped the microphone sending three booming echoes through the ballroom. "If the ladies would stay put on the dance floor or make their way over if not there already, it's time for the bride to toss the bouquet as per tradition."

Oh, no.

Hannah immediately turned on her heel to leave. "That's both our cues to head back to the table," she said, not bothering to wait for him. She didn't get far. A feminine hand reached for her out of nowhere through the crowd and grabbed her by the forearm.

"Oh, no, you don't. Come back here." Hannah turned to find Mandy's maid of honor, who happened to also be her older sister, tugging her back onto the dance floor.

"Come on, Hannah," Lexie said on a trail of

laughter. "We all know you're probably going to be next. May as well catch the bouquet and make it official."

Clearly, she hadn't heard about Hannah's broken relationship. But why would she? It wasn't the type of thing one announced while attending a celebration.

Hannah suppressed a groan. The last thing she wanted to do was stand here and explain to Mandy's sister exactly why it was such a horrifying thought that she try and catch the bouquet.

For one, her relationship was no more.

For another, she was already married!

How in the world would she even begin to explain any of that? She couldn't. Instead, she faked a smile and tightly followed Lexie back to the center of the dance floor. But not before catching an apologetic look from Alden who looked abashed on her behalf. Hannah could only shrug his way in resignation.

From the front of the crowd of ladies, Mandy let out a squeal of a laugh, then turned around and flung the bouquet behind her. Hannah watched in horror as it arched through the air in her direction. She could have sworn at one point it hung suspended in midair before it began to fall. It hit her square in the chest.

Hannah had no choice but to catch it.

* * *

Alden didn't know whether to laugh or groan out loud as he watched the bouquet head straight for Hannah and land in her hands. He knew the last thing she'd wanted was to be the one to catch those flowers.

Mandy had turned and was clapping with delight upon seeing where her aim had landed. Or was *target* a more appropriate word?

He began to pull Hannah's chair out, he'd already swung by the bar and procured two glasses of a bubbly cocktail for the two of them. But before Hannah could turn and make her way back, Max strode to his wife's side.

He had the microphone in his hands. "Now it's time for the gentlemen," he declared, then unclipped his boutonniere from his lapel. "It's only fair that one of the fellas gets a chance and then we can have a couples dance with the two winners."

Before Max had even gotten the last word out, close to a dozen men began making their way toward the dance floor. Hannah's jaw had dropped, a look of sheer horror plastered on her face. One of those men would get the chance to dance with Hannah.

Not if Alden could help it.

Setting the drinks down so abruptly they almost spilled, he shrugged off his jacket and strode toward the dance floor. Hannah caught his gaze and flashed him a smile he wouldn't be able to describe. Relief, mixed with gratitude. And something else.

Alden got there just in time as the boutonniere came flying out of Max's hand. Without much thought, he jumped into the air with both hands raised and a fervent prayer on his lips.

He'd never been much of a praying man but somehow it worked. When he landed, the boutonniere was securely in his left hand.

Max actually winked at him once he turned back around. He motioned toward the band that began playing a slow jazzy number, which Alden assumed to be his cue. Walking over to Hannah with what he hoped was a reassuring smile, he stretched his arms out and waited until she stepped into them.

"I think we may have been set up," he said into her ear as she reached her hands around his shoulders.

"I'd say there's a good chance that's true."

"Looks like the next dance is ours, sweetheart." He pulled her close against him and they began to sway to the music.

He'd called her sweetheart. Why that endearment sent her heart thudding, Hannah couldn't guess. No doubt Alden had simply thrown it out carelessly. There wasn't any kind of real weight or affection behind the term.

He was a charmer. He always had been. She couldn't succumb to that charm now, of all times. She had a broken heart to mend, a life to get back to that was going to look significantly different than what she'd lived the past few months. Her confusing feelings for her high school crush had no part in trying to pull that life together.

She knew there were dozens of eyes trained on the pair of them. But somehow Hannah felt as if she and Alden were the only two people in the room. The scent of him wrapped around her like a warm comfortable blanket on a snowy day. She could feel his heartbeat through her skin at every point their bodies made contact. She couldn't have imagined why Max and Mandy might have planned this, if they even had. But for the life of her, she couldn't find any regret that this moment was happening.

Through her peripheral vision, she saw other couples join them on the dance floor. But they may as well not even exist. Right now, it was just the two of them and the music that surrounded them.

She knew she hadn't imagined it when he pulled her tighter against his length. Hannah wondered what might have happened if she and

Alden were alone together and things between them were somehow different. Might Alden have kissed her?

Heaven help her, she would have let him. Maybe she might have even been the one to instigate the kiss. She couldn't be sure whether to be relieved they were surrounded by others or wish they would all disappear somehow.

How was this happening? How had her childhood crush on Alden grown into some kind of fantasy full of longing?

Was she just broken because she'd lost Justin?

The answer to that was almost embarrassingly clear. She'd dodged a bullet. If she could feel so much attraction to another man within days of their breakup, getting engaged to Justin clearly would have been a colossal mistake.

So what was she going to do about this inconvenient attraction to Alden? Further complicated by the fact that she was actually married to the man?

That telltale little devil popped up out of nowhere again.

Why don't you just enjoy yourself for just one night? Worry about all the rest later.

Hannah resisted the strong urge to literally brush an imaginary piece of lint off her shoulder to remove the imaginary rascal who seemed to lead her straight into trouble so often.

The song came to an end all too soon. With great reluctance, she moved to step out of Alden's embrace, the bouquet of flowers still clutched in her hand.

Alden held onto her for just a beat longer than was necessary. The idea of it sent a jolt of electricity rushing through her system. Was he as affected by their dance as much as she was?

She wanted to know the answer so badly. But there was no way she could come out and ask.

Max appeared at their side, a mischievous grin spread over his bearded face. Hannah was torn between thanking the other man and attempting to throttle him. Her emotions were a jumbled mess.

The music turned bouncy fast with a song she recognized as a classic rock and roll tune. If memory served, the high school football team always played the song at home games. It was the one the team rushed out onto the field to while it sounded loudly from the gymnasium speakers.

One by one, Max's brothers materialized next to him and Alden. Hannah took the opportunity to rush away. She needed some air.

"Hannah," Alden's voice sounded softly behind her but she pretended not to hear. A glance back a moment later told her he'd been pulled in by the other men and was now performing some kind of complicated dance routine they all seemed to know.

She took a moment to watch, unable to tear her eyes off Alden.

What had just happened?

Why was her heart pounding, her pulse racing? Why had she been loath to leave Alden's embrace?

It was just a simple dance. She shouldn't have been so affected. Hannah stepped out into the sidewalk and took a deep breath. She had to get a grip. In less than forty-eight hours, they would be splitting paths and perhaps never see each other again.

First, they had to get that divorce.

When she returned to the ballroom a few minutes later, Alden was already back at the table. He immediately stood up as she approached.

"Hey, I was wondering where you'd run off to."

If he'd been as affected by their dance, he was doing a great job of not showing it. She could only hope her own demeanor appeared as carefree. She flashed him an exaggerated smile. "Just needed some fresh air."

The rest of the evening went by in a blur.

Hannah made sure the only dancing they did from then on was fast and involved no touching.

By the time the bride and groom bid a cheerful goodbye to their guests to prepare for their honeymoon, the evening was swiftly coming to a close. Hannah's feet hurt and her emotions were no less chaotic.

"I think I might be ready to call it a night."

Alden nodded and retrieved his jacket from the back of the chair. "I'll walk you up to your room."

It was hard not to stare at him. All the dancing had lent a robust color to his cheeks; he'd undone the top several buttons of his collared shirt and rolled up his sleeves. The man really was a pleasure to look at. It was hard to get her fill.

She forced her gaze away and stood, following him out of the ballroom and into the elevator across the lobby.

When they reached her floor and made it to her door, she knew better than to invite him in. The temptation to ask him to stay might be too great to fight. As it was, the sheer magnitude of his allure was tempting her beyond comfort. But this was as good an opportunity as any to give him his ring back.

"Thanks, Alden. I had fun tonight," she began.

"If you'll just wait here a moment, I've been meaning to give you the ring back."

He surprised her by arguing. "I'd like you to keep it."

"Alden, that's very generous, but I couldn't do that. It's worth too much. Let me go get it for you."

He reached for her, stopped her before she could open the door. "Look, there's something I want to run by you."

His eyes were focused on her face, his mouth tight. Whatever this something was that he wanted to discuss, it was weighing on his mind.

Hannah leaned her back against the doorframe. "All right. What is it."

He shook his head, crammed his hands into his pockets. "Not now. It's been a long couple of days."

She couldn't argue with that. Between her tumultuous emotions and the chaos of the past forty-eight hours, Hannah wasn't sure she had the wherewithal to consider anything Alden might want to discuss.

"Meet me for breakfast tomorrow," he continued. "We can talk about the ring then."

What was there to talk about? She'd assumed they'd get together at some point tomorrow to figure out what to do about a divorce.

But this sounded like something else. What in the world did he have in mind?

The curiosity alone was enough to help make her decision. "Sure, let's have breakfast."

Alden hoped he knew what he was doing. And he hoped Hannah would agree to his proposal. He just wasn't quite sure how he was going to go about asking her.

The time he'd spent with Hannah at the wedding last night had been one of the most memorable evenings of his life. He might describe it as magical. Not a feeling he'd had too often after spending time with a woman. If that made him a newly minted romantic of some sort, then he was more than ready to accept it. Dancing with her had sealed it. The idea vaguely roaming around in his head had taken full form after holding her in his arms while swaying to the music.

As preposterous as it might sound, he had to ask her. He'd never forgive himself if he didn't.

He could approach this as just another business proposal. Funny he couldn't recall ever being this nervous at a business presentation before, not even some of the more relevant ones. Somehow, the stakes here were even higher. Though he'd be hard pressed to say why.

The worse that could happen is that she would

laugh and then say no. Leaving him no worse off, really. There was absolutely no reason to be as nervous as he was.

He'd suggested a diner rather than the elaborate buffet at their resort hotel. No doubt many of the wedding attendees would be there to eat and the last thing he needed were friends or acquaintances around to watch all this go down.

He led Hannah to an open booth and took a seat across from her. A server wearing a '50s-style uniform complete with a white lace apron and a cute bonnet appeared immediately with two personal-sized steaming carafes.

"Thank you, you're an angel," Hannah declared to the other woman, reaching for the coffee right away.

"Rough night?" Alden asked after the chuckling waitress had walked away.

Hannah took a sip of coffee without bothering with any cream or sugar. "I didn't get much sleep. How about you?"

He'd hardly gotten any himself, warring thoughts keeping him awake most of the night. Weighing the merits of his idea with the utter ridiculousness of how it was going to sound on the surface when he got it all out.

Hannah took another sip and reached for her purse. She pulled out a small velvet box he had no problem recognizing.

"Here, before I forget. Take the ring back."

He held up a hand when she reached it out to him. "Hannah, I really think you should keep it."

Her eyes grew wide. "Alden, we went over this last night. I can't keep something so valuable. I can't imagine a single reason why I should. Or why you would even suggest such a thing. Unless…"

Alden's pulse jumped, could she possibly have guessed what he wanted to do?

The next instant, Hannah's hand clenched tight on top of the table. "Is this another attempt at an apology? You don't have to try and buy me off for a mistake we both made together."

Whoa. Not only had she guessed wrong, now she was offended and angry. It was not the way he'd intended this conversation to start. So he didn't give himself a chance to think or agonize any longer. Alden went ahead and blurted the real reason he didn't want to take the ring back.

"I'd like for us to stay married."

CHAPTER SIX

SHE COULDN'T HAVE possibly heard him right. "I beg your pardon." She laughed before being able to ask the next question. "I could have sworn you just said you wanted to stay married. I couldn't have really heard that, right?"

He didn't answer, simply continued to stare at her.

Holy heaven. She *had* heard right. And Alden had meant what he said.

Okay. This was a bit of a curve ball. One she clearly hadn't seen coming. She rubbed her fingers over her forehead to dispel some of the tension that had suddenly pooled there. She really didn't have time for this. A slew of decisions and to-dos awaited her back home. Her mother didn't even know about her breakup, for heaven's sake. That wasn't a conversation she was looking forward to. Oh, then there was the whole need to find another job because she couldn't stomach the thought of going to the office every day to work with her ex.

"Alden, if this is some kind of joke…"

He held his hands out, palms up. "Look, I didn't mean to blurt it out that way."

As if his delivery were the problem. "Why would you even think to say it at all?"

"I really have thought this through. If you'd just hear me out."

She didn't get a chance to respond as the waitress came back to take their order at that very moment. Her gaze shifted from the ring on the center of the table, then to the two of them. "Should I come back?"

"That would be great," Alden said while at the very same moment Hannah answered with, "No, I'm ready to order."

Their waitress pursed her lips before looking at him questioningly. He gestured toward Hannah. "Go ahead. And whatever she orders, make it two. I'll have the same."

"I'll have the tower of chocolate chip pancakes with extra whipped cream and chocolate syrup. And a side of candied walnuts."

Alden winced at her choice across the table.

"Coming right up with two," the waitress said, then pivoted away.

"I think I got a cavity in one of my molars just hearing you place that order."

Hannah wasn't about to admit that a small petty part of her had deliberately chosen a breakfast she knew he would have never picked for himself. Her mood had soured beyond reason. What exactly was he about to tease her with? The notion that they could stay married made absolutely no sense.

Didn't it?

She needed more coffee. Maybe a gallon more. "Alden, are you playing with me?" she asked him as she poured more into her mug. This time she doctored it with plenty of cream and a dollop of sugar.

"On the contrary."

"Then what exactly is happening here?"

He leaned over across the table, pulled the ring out of its box and studied it. "This is just a symbol. A talisman."

"And?"

"It doesn't necessarily have to represent a real union. Neither does a piece of paper signed by an official."

Hannah merely repeated the simple word yet again. "And?"

"It just so happens we got married the other night. And it also just so happens that I could really use a wife for my next business venture."

Hannah felt her jaw drop as Alden continued, "If you prefer, you can look at this as a simple job offer."

Business. Job. He was speaking in puzzles now. For the life of her, she couldn't seem to make any of the pieces fit.

"Let me explain," he said, pouring himself some coffee.

"I wish you would."

"I'm trying to form a partnership with a very traditional family in a rather conservative part of the world. The only other parties in consideration, my only competition, are stable family men."

"How can that possibly matter in this day and age?"

"I assure you, in many parts of the world, it still matters very much. I know for a fact I'm being viewed as a less viable option because of my status as a single man."

And also because of his reputation as a hard partying bachelor. Hannah didn't voice the thought out loud. Something told her Alden already knew that aspect about him was also playing a factor with the people he was trying to do business with overseas.

He continued to explain. "I fly out again in three days for more negotiations. I'm proposing you come with me. As my wife. Which, technically, you happen to be."

As his wife. Which she was. Three days.

No!

It was out of the question. Why was she even entertaining anything he was saying?

"Look, I have a life I have to get back to. I can't just drop everything and travel to the other end of the world with you. I'm supposed to fly back to Boston tomorrow night where my mom will be waiting for me, at which point I'll have to break the news to her that rather than getting engaged, I actually broke up with my almost-fiancé. The next day I have to go into a job where my ex will also be, and if you don't think that's going to be awkward, you're not thinking. And if you guessed that also means that I should start looking for another job, clap for yourself. Because that's absolutely correct."

She felt nearly out of breath by the time she finished. Alden actually had the nerve to chuckle. Hannah resisted the urge to toss a packet of sugar at him. "What exactly is funny about any of that?"

He leaned back, crossed his arms in front of his chest. "Because everything you're saying just helps to make my point that this is a good idea. For both of us." He began counting on his fingers. "One, you don't have to tell your mom your relationship fell apart, instead you can tell her you decided you're doing some traveling.

Two, you don't have to go back to a job you don't enjoy, which happens to also employ a man you don't want to see."

Their food arrived, sparing Hannah the need to answer. She hated that he was actually making sense. And she had to admit, some of the points he made were actually worthy of consideration.

"There's something else you might want to consider," he added, pulling his plate closer and poking a fork into the bottom pancake.

"What's that?"

"We'd be traveling to one of the textile capitals of the world. Istanbul has the grand bazaar, which sells everything from silk to handmade rugs to fashion jewelry. Shopping in the Aegean boasts some of the most renowned boutiques and fashion houses. If you ever considered changing your career to one that involved designing and creating clothing, you'd find inspiration there like nowhere else."

Hannah paused.

Alden must have sensed the slowly forming cracks in her resolve. "Of course, I'll pay you for your time," he told her. "Consider it getting paid while you do some research about your next career move."

Hannah's head began to spin. Her life was about logic and numbers and order. Aside from when she designed her clothing. That was the only time she let her imagination and creativity take over.

There was nothing logical about the offer Alden just made her. Yet, somehow there was.

She had no clue how to decide. And she only had three days.

Maybe all the sugar had gone to his head. But he could swear Hannah was wavering. He had to balance on a very precarious high wire, like those stunt performers so well-known in this city. On the one hand, he wanted to press while he glimpsed a slight advantage. But this had to be wholly Hannah's decision. He couldn't push. He could only lay out all the ways this deal would benefit them both and hope she came around.

She suddenly set her fork down. "You know, I'm not much of a gambler."

Uh-oh. That statement didn't really bode well, now did it?

She continued, "But I was thinking of hitting the slots once more before we leave Las Vegas."

"The slots?" What did playing the slots have to do with anything? Was she deliberately changing the subject?

She took a slow sip of coffee. Then another. Alden stayed silent, just waiting. She had to be going somewhere with this. Though for the life of him, he couldn't figure out where. She bit another forkful of pancake before answering and he lost his concentration for a moment as he gazed at her rich ruby lips.

Focus.

"I'm not sure how to respond to your offer just yet."

That lent him a small amount of hope. She was saying no outright.

"This would all be completely friendly," he told her. "We wouldn't actually…" He cleared his throat, there was no non-awkward way to say this. "That is, I mean, it would be completely platonic."

She lifted her shoulder in a gesture that said, *Duh*... "That goes without saying."

Yeah, maybe. He figured he should say it anyway. "What do you think? Up for an adventure?"

She chewed some more, left the question unanswered for so long that he thought she planned to completely ignore it. Finally, she set her fork down and blew out a long breath. "Let's leave it to chance, shall we?"

"How do you propose we do that?"

She shrugged. "We're in the city of games of chance. Let's let one of those games decide whether I accept your offer or not."

She reached for her purse, pulled out several bills and placed them on the table. "Breakfast is on me."

Then she stood and motioned for him to follow her out of the diner.

What choice did he have but to grab the ring, then follow her out?

Less than five minutes later, they were walking through the gaming hall of one of the larger casinos on the strip. Hannah hadn't said much on the way over here, but she certainly strode down the sidewalk with no small amount of determination.

"This one should work, plenty of empty slots," she said, looking around, the sounds of pings and bells and electronic ringing echoed through the air. He could only watch as she walked over to the window and exchanged several bills for two buckets of chips. She returned to his side and handed him one of the buckets with a smile. "Also on me."

Okay.

"Uh…thanks. But what are we really doing here?"

"Killing two birds with one stone."

"How, exactly?"

"We'll both play these slots. And we'll keep playing until one of us wins something. Anything. It could be less than a dollar. Still a win."

"What happens then?" he asked, though he figured he could guess.

"I win first, I go back to my formerly dull yet familiar life that's now suddenly tumultuous and uncertain."

She shook the bucket of chips before continuing. "You win, I come on this trip with you. And pretend to be your wife."

"You are my wife."

She poked him in the chest. "You need to stop saying that. Even though it's true."

"Can't we just flip a coin or something?"

"That wouldn't be terribly exciting now, would it? It's playing the slots to decide or my answer is no now."

He could merely stare at her in astonishment. "This is really how you want to make the decision?"

She shrugged. "As good a way as any. I'm just going to let fate decide for me."

Alden followed as she walked down the aisle and picked an empty machine. Joker's Wild said the neon sign flashing above it. He sat down at the one next to her. He was down to about half the bucket of chips when he pulled the arm and watched as three rows of bright red cherries lined up perfectly on the bright red line on the screen and the machine went wild.

Not quite the jackpot. But he'd hit a winning pull.

Next to him, Hannah jumped up and shook her head, disbelieving.

"I guess that settles it then, sweetheart."

She looked at him with acceptance and resignation. And if his mind wasn't deceiving him, maybe even a hint of excitement in her eyes.

"A deal is a deal," she said on a sigh.

Alden resisted the urge to pump his fist in the air, waited for the attendant to arrive to verify his winnings.

Hannah leaned over to study his machine. "It's still ringing and the lights are still flashing."

"That's because I just won several thousand dollars, sweetheart. All yours. Consider it a starting bonus."

CHAPTER SEVEN

Three days later

IF SOMEONE HAD told her a month ago that she'd be traveling via Alden's private jet to Istanbul as his pretend yet real wife, she would have asked them what romantic fantasy novel they'd been reading.

The sentence she'd just thought seemed straight out of a movie or book. Yet, here she was, walking up the steps to be greeted by a uniformed flight attendant and a dapper-looking pilot awaiting them in the main cabin.

"I can't say I've ever flown private before. This will be quite the experience."

When exactly had Alden become so successful? She knew he was a recognized name over in the hospitality industry. He'd manage to achieve a truly impressive level of success for someone so relatively young.

"I want to make sure you're comfortable,"

he said. "Anything you need, ask Sandra. We should touch down in a few short hours."

"Thank you. I will. I might just indulge in a nap, however." It wasn't until she'd sat down in the leather swivel bucket seat that she realized just how tired she was. The past couple of days, ever since the wedding, her life had been a whirlwind of activity and major changes.

She'd packed up her apartment and given notice at her job and finally took advantage of all the vacation days she'd let accumulate. It helped that she'd made sure to finish up her projects before the wedding.

And she'd turned Justin down flat each time he'd made noises about getting together to just "talk" about their undone relationship. As far as she was concerned, there was nothing to talk about.

"What did your mother think about you being away?" Alden asked, studying her.

She shrugged. "I might have been rather vague about my reasons for leaving."

Alden lifted an eyebrow in question. "Let's just say she made her own assumptions about what kind of business trip this was."

He tilted his head toward her. "And you let her make them."

"That's right." There would be time to explain to Mama later. And she'd certainly have quite a bit of explaining to do.

"After that, it was only a matter of moving out of the apartment, then finalizing things at work. Aside from Mama, there was no one else to even inform. No one else who might even miss me while I'm gone."

Womp-womp. That comment dangerously bordered on self-pity.

"No one?" Alden asked.

Hannah shook her head. "Not even a pet." She curled her legs under her lap. "Not that the lack of one was my choice."

"No?"

Hannah shook her head. "Justin was allergic to cats and had declared that he'd never been a dog person." Now that they were over, it gave Hannah pause at just how incompatible she and Justin actually were—if one looked hard enough.

"That's too bad," Alden said. "Didn't you have a golden tabby back when we were in school?"

It surprised her that he remembered the small detail. "That's right. Tabeetha."

"Clever."

She chuckled. "I loved that furry little fluff ball. And I would have loved to come home to a tail-wagging puppy. Or a whiskered kitten. I love dogs. But I've always been partial to cats."

"Then you're going to love the time you're in Istanbul."

Before she could ask what he meant by that, Alden's phone rang on the wooden table between them.

"Excuse me, I need to take this if you don't mind."

She nodded and he rose to stride to the other end of the plane to take the call. Hannah took the opportunity to study him as he spoke. They'd communicated rather sporadically over the past few days, then this morning a limo had arrived at her apartment to drive her to the airport. In the meantime, he'd deposited a sizable amount into her bank account. Several times over the amount he'd procured at the casino slots that day.

What had she been thinking to leave such a major decision to such a fluky random act of chance? She'd never been so impulsive. But then, Alden sure seemed to bring out the impulsive side of her. She'd actually married him that way.

Now she watched as he shifted the phone from one ear to the other as he spoke. He'd come a long way from that cheery young teenage boy who'd pretty much had to raise himself after both his parents had left him to his own devices at the ripe old age of fifteen.

She couldn't imagine what that must have been like for him. Her own mother was overly vocal about her opinions and was definitely a meddler. She could be overbearing and opinionated. But Hannah had never felt lacking in parental love.

Unlike Alden who'd essentially been abandoned by both parents. First, his mom, then his father shortly after. Look how far Alden had come despite all the unfair cards he'd been dealt in life.

Her eyes began to droop and she could no longer fight her exhaustion. Alden was still speaking on the phone when she drifted off to sleep.

When her lids fluttered open again, she had no idea how long she'd been asleep. Alden was back in his chair across from her, hunched over the table between them, typing into a sleek black laptop.

He looked up before she could avert her gaze. Caught red-handed watching him. The corners of his lips lifted into a smile.

"What?"

She shook her head, uncurled her legs from underneath her. "Nothing. Just observing how driven you are. You're doing so much to ensure this deal goes through."

He shrugged. "I don't know how else to be.

If you go hungry often enough as a kid, you work hard to avoid having it happen to you as an adult." His lips thinned as soon as he said the last word, as if he regretted what he'd just told her.

Hungry. Hannah would never have guessed. Everyone in town knew about Alden's situation. They knew his parents had left him alone in that house that they'd paid for outright when Alden was just born. But a teenage boy needed so much more than a roof over his head.

"There was no one else to make sure the bills got paid so that the water ran and the lights stayed on," he said, not quite meeting her eyes.

"Why didn't you sell the house, Alden?"

He shrugged. "It wasn't mine to sell. And a fifteen-year-old walking into a real estate office to inquire about a sale might have raised a few eyebrows and a good amount of suspicion. I didn't need the authorities digging into my circumstances and then leading me straight into the foster system."

She'd had no idea. It was hard to know what to say. The whole town, except for Max's family, had pretty much left Alden Hamid alone. Including her and her mother. The fact that they'd had their own troubles at the time was no excuse.

And here she was complaining that she didn't have a pet to come home to.

His eyes darted around her face, then he leaned back and crossed his arms over his chest. His whole demeanor had suddenly shut down.

"No need to look at me that way, Hannah."

"What way?"

"With such sorrow. I don't need anyone's pity."

He couldn't have read her reaction more wrong. She hadn't meant to insult him. Just the opposite.

"I'm sorry. I didn't mean to."

"The Harpers made sure I got at least two or three square meals a week." He was referring to Max's family. "But they had their own several mouths to feed. As for the rest, I managed to scrape by."

He certainly had. No small accomplishment.

"I know you did," she told him. "And I absolutely didn't mean any offense. If anything, what you're seeing on my face is pure admiration."

His eyebrows shot up clear to his hairline. She'd shocked him.

Well, she'd shocked herself. But she wasn't sorry. She'd said what she'd said and she meant it.

* * *

The afternoon sun had begun to give way to evening by the time they touched down at Istanbul International Airport. The car his administrative assistant had arranged for them awaited outside by the curb. Within minutes, their driver was zigzagging through the busy streets on their way to the hotel.

Alden stole a glance at Hannah sitting next to him in the back seat. She couldn't seem to tear her gaze away from the view outside. He could hardly blame her. Istanbul was a bustling city, busy at all hours with both locals and tourists crowding its meandering sidewalks and hilly streets.

"I can't wait to explore this city," Hannah declared, turning away from the window to face him. Excitement was practically dripping from her features. "Please say we'll have time."

"We'll make certain of it," he reassured her. "What kind of hus—" He caught himself before he could finish the word. It was better to view each other as business partners more so than anything else. He began again, "What kind of business associate would I be if I brought you to Istanbul but then didn't take you to see the sights?"

Hannah actually clapped twice before turning back to stare out the window. Alden studied her profile with a smile. As cliché as it was, she appeared to be a kid viewing the glass case in a candy store.

Luckily, any awkwardness from the tense conversation during the flight over seemed to be past them. He knew he'd edged perilously close to snapping at her. He just wasn't used to discussing his past too often. Such talk brought to the surface all manner of painful memories he'd long ago buried and preferred to keep that way.

He'd known as a kid the way the townsfolk talked about him. He knew they referred to him as the poor Hamid kid who'd been abandoned by both parents. No one had been outwardly cruel. And the Harpers had made sure he'd had what he needed to graduate high school and then attend college on a scholarship and countless loans. But if he never returned to Reardon again in this lifetime, it would be too soon.

So he'd been short with Hannah, careless with his response. Then she'd said she admired his determination. No, she'd actually said she'd admired *him*. No one had ever said such words to him before. Darned if he'd been able to come up with a response. The whole conversation had thrown him off and he was happy it was behind them.

The driver finally turned onto a side street

and stopped the car. Hannah looked at him questioningly. "A lot of these streets in the Sultanahmet area are pedestrian and trolley only. We'll have to walk the rest of the way to our hotel. Levin will make sure our bags make their way to our room."

The driver opened her door and tipped his hat to her. "I'll be sure you get your luggage right away, miss."

Alden took her by the elbow and they made their way into the throng of the crowd—shoppers, partiers, those out for an evening snack.

"I feel like I'm in a whole new world," Hannah said, her eyes darting from one area to another as they made their way through the square. The evening was balmy and warm, a myriad of scents in the air. How often had he walked through this square and not appreciated any of it the way Hannah so clearly was. The smile on her face appeared as if it might permanently be etched on her lips.

"We can come back down after getting settled in, if you'd like."

Funny, not less than twenty minutes ago, Alden was ready to crash in the hotel suite with a hot tea followed by a long shower, then sleep. He'd had no intention of heading back out. But the look on Hannah's face as she took in their surroundings somehow gave him a second wind. He wanted to see that look for as long as she held it.

"I'd love that! Yes. Without question."

"Somehow I knew that would be your answer."

"I was so afraid you wouldn't offer."

He chuckled, led her closer to their hotel. "Let's go get freshened up first. My regular suite happens to be on the south side of the resort. Prime viewing."

"Of what?" she asked, slowing to admire a vendor's rack of silk scarves and *örtüs*.

"The Hagia Sophia. You won't believe your eyes when you see it all lit up from the balcony."

"Our suite has a balcony overlooking the great Hagia Sophia?"

He nodded with another chuckle. "I mean, it might not compare to the fake Eiffel Tower we had a view of back in Vegas."

She punched him on the arm playfully. "Are you trying to compare a man-made tourist structure in the middle of a desert gambling town to one of the greatest architectural creations in the world?"

He laughed at her horrified expression. Vegas and the wedding already seemed like a lifetime ago. Images of the night they'd gotten married had gradually spotted his brain over the past few days. Though they hadn't been intimate in the physical sense, they'd spent the night in each other's arms. He may not have remembered much from that evening but he certainly remembered the way Hannah had felt in his embrace. The scent of her hair under his nose. Her warm breath against his bare chest.

They'd kissed. He couldn't even say if he remembered or was conjuring from his imagination, but he recollected the taste of strawberries and vanilla when he'd had his mouth on hers. Her hot breath intermingling with his as he explored her mouth with his tongue. A ball of heat curled in his middle.

Stop it.

He couldn't even allow himself to think such thoughts. He'd made it clear to her that this was nothing more than a business venture in which he needed her help. He couldn't let himself forget that.

Hannah's senses hummed on overload as she shut off the shower and stepped out of the stall. Wrapping a thick Turkish towel around her middle, she checked her reflection in the mirror. Despite the hours of traveling internationally—it was an entirely different experience to fly privately with access to exclusive lounges—she felt alert and full of energy. And excitement. It was just such a novel experience for her to be here in such a foreign-to-her place.

When was the last time she'd felt this excited about anything? She couldn't recall. She could barely remember the last trip she'd taken. A weeklong trip to the Florida Keys with Justin and his family. Hannah had spent more time with his mother than she actually had with Justin. He and his father had boarded a boat daily, rain or shine, to deep-sea fish.

The Keys were fun in a subdued kind of way. But Istanbul was an entirely different vibe. She'd never been anywhere this exotic. The streets they'd driven through had seemed a cross between stylish Newbury Street in Boston and something out of a scene from an Aladdin or Sinbad movie. She couldn't wait to get back out there and explore as much as she could during the short time they had here.

One thing was certain, once all this was over and Alden had his deal in hand, she was going to find a way to come back here. Maybe she'd bring her mom. A pang of sorrow settled in the pit of her stomach. The next time she'd come here, Alden wouldn't be accompanying her.

Stepping out of the bathroom and into her private room, she headed over to the closet where she'd unpacked her clothing earlier. Alden's suite at this hotel appeared to be an entire floor complete with two separate bedrooms with their own bathroom and shower. Funny, she hadn't even thought to ask him about the accommodations to make sure she'd have her privacy. She'd assumed Alden would make sure she'd have it. And he had.

Picking out a pair of comfortable cotton capris and a fluid three-quarter-length colorful top, she quickly got dressed, then grabbed a sweater and her cross-body purse. When she made it out to the common sitting area between their rooms, Alden was already out there dressed and seated on the black leather L-shaped couch. The large screen television played an intense-looking soccer match with the announcer rambling loudly and quickly. Alden didn't really seem to be paying attention to it though, he had his laptop open on his lap with a look of focused concentration on his face.

A muscle fluttered in the vicinity of her chest as he stood and smiled at her. The man really knew how to wear his clothes well. Black pressed casual slacks that accented his hips with a short-sleeved Henley the color of an ocean sky that brought out the hue of his eyes and the tanned muscular skin of his arm. Lordy, she couldn't even remember noticing a man's arms before, let alone appreciating how muscular they might be.

He looked like he'd just stepped out of a men's cologne ad.

"Ready to go?" he asked, setting the laptop down on the coffee table and shutting the cover.

"Absolutely."

He looked her over. "You look nice." He turned away as soon as he said it, as if the words had slipped out unbidden. "I mean, what you're wearing is very appropriate given we'll be walking around a square of shops and vendors for a bit before dinner."

"Dinner?" Hannah had just assumed they'd grab a bite from one of the many food carts she'd noticed along the way. All of them had made her mouth water with the spicy, tangy aroma that wafted her way as she passed each one.

"I took the liberty of having a table reserved at one of my favorite spots nearby in a couple hours. The food is amazing. Hope that's okay?"

"Sounds great. Thank you for doing that."

"You're welcome."

"Shall we go, then?" Hannah wasn't going to bother hiding her eagerness.

"Just one thing." He stepped closer to her. The scent of his now-familiar aftershave did something to her insides whenever she smelled it.

Before she could guess what he was doing,

he reached into his pocket and pulled out a very recognizable velvet box. Hannah's breath caught as he flipped open the box with one hand and took her arm with the other.

"You're going to need this again," he said, his breath warm against her cheek. "May as well start wearing it now." Her hand shook as he slipped it on her finger. There was no way he hadn't noticed. Hopefully, he would chalk it up to her excitement about being in this city rather than the truth. That the whole scenario was taking her mind and heart on a journey that would be perilous in all manner of ways.

Like imagining what it would feel like if this man were really slipping a ring on her finger because he'd just proposed to her, legitimately and soberly this time.

Somehow, she found her voice enough to answer. "Uh…yeah. I guess that makes sense." Incredibly, her voice was hardly shaky at all as she spoke.

When she looked up at Alden, he was staring at her with an intensity that had her knees wobbling. Hannah pulled her hand out of his with a bit too much speed.

Get a grip.

The ring on her finger may be a valuable diamond on a platinum band, but it might as well be costume jewelry. Because that's exactly what it was, just part of a costume for a role she was playing. It was like how those actresses walking the red carpet at all those events always wore those absurdly expensive baubles they had to return the day after. This wasn't any different.

Some day in the near future, she'd be returning this ring back to Alden yet again.

CHAPTER EIGHT

ALDEN WILLED THE elevator to somehow go faster down to the lobby because the silence between him and Hannah now was almost deafening.

He'd held her hand a little too long up there when he'd slipped the diamond ring back on Hannah's finger. Now as a result, there was a slight tinge of awkwardness between them.

Just like back in school. He used to get so tongue-tied near Hannah, always at a loss for what to say. Or he'd somehow managed to say or do the wrong thing. The same way he had upstairs when he'd lingered holding her hand.

It was no wonder she was standing there still and barely blinking as she watched the panel of numbers above the elevator doors.

In his defense there'd been a lot happening in his head during that moment. The action must have triggered some of the memories hidden from the night they'd eloped. Images of the first time he'd given her the ring. He'd simply handed it to her then, he finally remembered. The two of them both doubled over in laughter. Hannah telling him they would have done just as well with a plastic ring from the gumball machine at the arcade they'd passed on the way to the chapel.

Alden released a sigh of relief when they finally arrived at the first-floor lobby and the elevator doors slid open.

The crowd had grown thicker in Sultanahmet Square when they stepped outside. The chords of oud music could be heard coming from more than one direction. A myriad of spoken languages sounded all around them. Outdoor cafés were full with customers, both those lingering over their afternoon tea or those who'd just arrived for an early dinner.

"I'm not quite sure what I was expecting but this definitely exceeds my imagination," Hannah said over his shoulder, following him toward the first row of shops.

"Hope you feel the same about dinner," he answered, opening the door of a ceramic shop. Hannah was sure to get a kick out of this place. It boasted an elaborate display of ceramic handmade cats in all sizes and colors.

"What do you mean?" she asked. "What's so special about dinner tonight?"

"Everything in Istanbul is special. And rarely

is any dinner simple. But you'll have to wait and see what I mean."

She looked like she wanted to press but was immediately distracted by the menagerie of cat ceramics. Her exclamation had him grinning.

"Oh, my, these are adorable." She fingered a small kitten figurine with long wire whiskers and a white spot over one eye. The thing looked so real, Alden half expected it to jump off the shelf and into Hannah's arms.

He couldn't help the grin that spread over his face at her reaction. It was just what he'd hoped for. "You said you've been wanting a kitten to come home to. Maybe you can start with a ceramic one for now."

Hannah actually squealed with delight. Delighting him in return. "I wish I could buy them all. Just ship every single one back to the States."

He chuckled. "As much as the shopkeeper would love that, how about we just start with one or two for now?"

Said shopkeeper appeared from the back room at that very moment.

"*Merhaba,*" she greeted them with a warm smile. "American?"

"*Merhaba,*" Alden returned her greeting with what he hoped was a passable accent. "Yes, good guess. American by way of New England."

"Welcome," the woman beamed. "I'm Ayse. Which ones would you like?" she asked Hannah directly, motioning to the shelf Hannah was still eyeing with sheer adoration.

Not for the first time, Alden had to appreciate the savvy of these shop owners. Always assuming the sale.

"It's so hard to decide," Hannah answered. "I wish I could take them all."

Alden tried not to wince. That was the kind of statement that was music to a shopkeeper's ears.

"Take as many as you like," Ayse said, her voice dripping with temptation. "We can ship them for you."

Hannah tilted her head, as if actually considering buying several. "Hmm. My own litter of adorable ceramic kittens."

If there was anything Alden knew about this city, it's that the people loved their cats.

Ayse turned her smile in his direction. "Your wife will be so happy with these."

Alden almost corrected her before he caught himself. Hannah really was his wife. There was no misinformation to correct.

"I'll take these three for now," Hannah said, pointing to what appeared to be a tomcat, a momma cat, and a baby kitten. "How much?"

The shopkeeper named an exorbitant amount.

Hannah appeared taken aback for a slight moment before she simply nodded, then reached for her purse.

Uh-oh. He hadn't told her about how customary it was to barter in this part of the world. From what little shopping he'd done last time he was here, Alden knew she was about to overpay more than twice what the items would normally sell for.

Ayse laughed and put a hand on Hannah's before she could pull her card out. "You're supposed to argue with me. Tell me that's too expensive. Make a show of leaving perhaps even."

Hannah blinked at the other woman before nodding slowly. "Gotcha. In that case, I think that's far too expensive. I refuse to pay so much."

The women play-argued for several more moments while Alden watched in amusement. So far, this trip was much more entertaining than his usual business trips. To add icing to the cake, he didn't have to order room service or grab a takeout box from the doner shop next door and bring it back to eat by himself as he appreciated the majestic sight of the Bosporus from his balcony alone.

The thought gave him pause.

Huh. He hadn't even realized doing things that way had been bothering him. Being alone in these cities was simply what he'd always done. But the thought of being here with anyone else wasn't meshing in his brain.

"I will not pay a penny more," Hannah said loudly with mock outrage, pulling him out of his thoughts.

The shopkeeper shook her head with a clearly exaggerated reaction. "Fine. Done. But you drive a hard bargain, Miss Hannah." The woman would have been much more convincing if her lips weren't trembling with unreleased laughter.

She turned her green kohl-lined eyes to Alden. "Your wife did good," she said. "You should be proud to have married her."

She would never get used to being referred to as Alden's wife. Not that there was any point in trying to get used to it. It wasn't as if the title was any kind of permanent, or even long-term, status.

"I could rush those back to the hotel room if you'd like." Alden pointed to the box she carried that held her precious newly prized possessions: a family of colorful ceramic cats. "So you don't have to carry that box around."

Hannah immediately shook her head to turn down his offer. Maybe it was silly of her, but she didn't want anything to break the momentum of this magical evening. She wanted it to continue unimpeded and uninterrupted with Alden by her side throughout.

"I think I'll be all right. I might need to buy one of those woven handbags over at that stall though to put them in."

"Looking to hone your bartering skills some more, are you?"

"I'm just getting started," she said with an exaggerated wave of her hand. Though the more reasonable, more logical part of her told her she should try and take it easy with the purchases. After all, money might be tight once she returned to the States. She was essentially unemployed, after all. Once this assignment, or whatever it could be called, with Alden was completed, she'd have to find another job.

Unless…she actually found enough inspiration during this trip to get started on sketching some designs. Enough to get started on a portfolio she might be able to shop around.

Could she really make it work? An entire career shift?

It seemed like such a pipe dream. Yet, Alden had made it sound quite achievable. Did she dare believe him?

Well, that's what she was here to find out. Already, her mind was spinning with ideas. Like maybe she'd draw a patterned dress the color of the Bosporus, intricately stitched with cat eyes along the hem and sleeves. Or maybe a pair of flowing wide pants that might work really well with the longer tunics hanging in some of the store windows.

"And where did you just drift off to?" Alden asked. "You walked right past the handbag store."

Huh. So she had.

"Sorry. There's just so much to see here," she said, backtracking her steps. Alden followed, shaking his head and smiling.

The handbag store was just as overwhelming. The colors and designs were so original and vibrant Hannah thought she might have stepped back into an animated movie again.

Two of the bags immediately caught her eye. One hand-stitched with ancient Ottoman lettering of intricate detail. The other a painted canvas of the Istanbul skyline accented with buttery soft leather. In the end, she just couldn't pick between the two. So she bought them both. Which of course just gave them yet more things to carry.

When they stepped out of the store, she turned to find Alden flexing his arms and doing pretend arm curls, straining with imaginary weights. When he finally stopped that, he wiped his brow as if overexerted, then took several gasping breaths. He looked ridiculous. More than one passerby gave an amused chuckle at his antics.

"What in the world are you doing?"

He tilted his head. "Just trying to get ready for all the shopping bags I'm certain to be carrying before you're through."

"Ha, ha. Very funny."

"Maybe we should have brought a cart."

Now they were even fake bickering like some really married couple. Teasing each other the way an actual married couple might.

Just stop it.

Hannah was ready to resume walking when Alden's expression completely changed. His playful smile vanished, his eyes narrowing on a distant target in the crowd. Hannah could feel him stiffening. The muscles around his jaw grew tight. Whatever Alden was looking at, he was not pleased.

She turned in the direction of his stare. But all she could see was the same scene all around—shoppers, diners, people roaming about, enjoying their day.

"Alden? What's wrong?"

He continued to stare for a bit longer before giving his head a brisk shake. Finally, he turned back to her.

"Nothing. I just thought I saw someone I know. I must have been mistaken."

Whoever he'd thought he'd seen, he didn't appear to be a fan.

He motioned for her to proceed and they'd only gone a few steps when Hannah's curiosity got the better of her.

"Who was it?"

He shook his head. "No one. It's not important."

That statement certainly didn't ring true given his reaction back there.

Alden was a successful businessman. Anyone with that level of success had to have made a few enemies along the way, deservedly or not. But the expression on Alden's face moments ago had been intense. Fierce almost. Her gut told her it was no business-related matter. It appeared much more personal.

Was there a woman in his past who had wounded him? So deeply that the mere possibility of seeing her had elicited such a jarring reaction? A sinking feeling churned in her middle at the thought. A feeling she refused to consider might be jealousy. She had no claim to Alden Hamid. No right to feel any kind of possessiveness.

She just had to keep reminding herself of that fact.

The fun and jovial mood of just moments ago was gone now. Replaced by a tension in the air that only seemed to grow with each step they took. It didn't help that Alden seemed to be scanning that same area in the distance every time she glanced back at him.

Hannah wanted so badly to find another way to ask for details but there seemed no good way to do so.

She paused in front of a crowded café. "Maybe we should just go back to the hotel," she said, her earlier happy mood now gone for good.

Alden appeared not to have even heard her. He was still too distracted.

The view was doing wonders for her state of mind. Hannah stepped over to the balcony railing and scanned the horizon. The Bosphoros was alight, framing the Hagia Sophia that stood majestically before it, the tall minarets shooting toward the sky above. She felt as if she might have stepped into a life-sized painting from the Byzantine era.

She'd made a beeline out here as soon as they'd arrived back at the suite after dropping her bags off on her bed.

Alden had immediately escaped himself and closed the door behind him after entering his own room with the explanation that he might as well get some work done until dinner. He'd encouraged Hannah to get some rest.

She wouldn't have imagined when they'd first stepped out earlier that this would be the way their evening might end. With both of them holed up in their own living quarters. Their excursion had started out so enjoyable and fun. But it was as if Alden's entire personality had changed after they'd left the handbag store.

So now, here she stood, admiring this wondrous view out here all by herself when she'd much rather be out there exploring it. With Alden by her side.

Wishful thinking. One would think she'd be over that penchant by now. Growing up without a father who'd abandoned them. Then being unceremoniously dumped by the man she'd wanted to marry.

Her limited experience with members of the opposite sex had been woefully less than ideal so far. What made her possibly think being with Alden would be any different?

He hadn't really wanted to marry her. If it weren't for this business prospect he was after, they'd be divorced already. The man hadn't even asked her out in high school, for heaven's sake. Despite having had countless opportunities to do so. He'd dated scores of other girls. But never her.

If it weren't for Max and Mandy's status as

their respective best friends, the two of them wouldn't have spent any time together at all.

Things were no different now. Hannah was still the girl who was there because it was convenient. Nothing more.

She wasn't sure how much time had passed when she heard the sliding glass door of the common balcony entrance swish open behind her. Alden appeared beside her a moment later.

"Is it time already for dinner?" she asked.

He draped his forearms on the balcony railing, his head slightly bowed with his gaze focused on the horizon.

"No, we still have some time," he answered. "Just thought I'd come out here and enjoy the scenery as well."

Hannah simply nodded. Did that mean he might be ready to talk to her finally? About exactly what had gotten him so rattled back there at the shopping bazaar?

Alden answered the question with his next words. "I know you must be curious about exactly what went down earlier. Why I acted the way I did."

She lifted her shoulder to answer. "It was rather uncharacteristic and sudden on your part."

He nodded slowly, not taking his gaze off

the horizon. "I get that. But I was hoping we could just enjoy the view for a few moments."

In silence was the implied remainder of that sentence.

"Of course," she answered. "It's not my place to pry, I know that. You don't owe me any kind of explanation." True enough. It wasn't as if she were really his wife. Why did she have to keep reminding herself of that so often?

If there was a woman out there who had broken his heart and left him so emotionally raw that the mere possibility of running into her changed his entire mood, it really was none of her business. Alden didn't really belong to her in any way. Not in heart. And not in body.

The fact that he didn't argue her last statement only proved her point.

A cover of clouds slowly moved over the night sky, darkening the balcony in shadows before either of them spoke again. Alden cleared his throat before he began. "There's been at least two occasions when I've traveled to this part of the world when I've run into my father."

Whatever Hannah had been expecting him to say, it certainly hadn't been that.

His father.

Her brain scrambled for a way to process what he'd just revealed. The last she'd heard, years ago, Alden's father had returned to his birthplace to a small village in Cyprus.

Alden continued, "I thought it might have happened again today," he added after several beats. "And I'm ashamed to admit that even after all these years, without any contact whatsoever, the possibility of seeing him again just throws me off." He sucked in a breath. "In any case, I'm sorry I let it ruin our first evening here."

For the life of her, Hannah couldn't think of a way to respond. Reflexively, she reached over to rest her hand on his forearm.

"You don't have to apologize to me. I'm the one who should tell you that I'm sorry."

He finally turned to her, blinking. "You? Whatever for?"

She struggled to find a way to answer. To put into words the jumble of thoughts scrambling through her brain. She should apologize for not giving him enough grace to explain it all in his own time. For jumping to a conclusion based solely on her own insecurities and the jealousy she had no business feeling. For selfishly worrying about her ruined evening rather than what Alden might be going through to have him react the way he had back there.

"Never mind," she answered. Maybe she'd be able to explain it to him at some point. But she couldn't summon the words right now. "Just want to say that you can talk to me if you want to. About anything." Hannah groaned inwardly. The words sounded so lame as she said them. So cliché. But it was the truth. Whatever this situation was between them, the whole fake marriage slash business arrangement. Beneath it all, they'd known each other for years. They'd both suffered the pain of abandonment by their fathers. On a deep-rooted level, they were friends. From where she was standing right now, that trumped all else.

"I appreciate that," Alden said, his voice thick. "But neither of my parents are topics I particularly enjoy discussing."

"Fair enough." She gave his arm a slight squeeze. "But I'm here if that ever changes." She meant that with her whole heart. Regardless of how this arrangement between them turned out in the end.

They stood silently, focused on the view for several more moments. How had it never occurred to her before just how much she and Alden had in common? The answer was simple. While both their fathers had abandoned them, at least Hannah had grown up with the benefit of having at least one devoted, committed parent, flawed as her mother may have been.

While Alden had been alone for years.

CHAPTER NINE

ALDEN FELT LIKE a fool. He'd only meant to go out there on the balcony to apologize to Hannah. Instead, she'd been compelled to try and comfort him, to assure him she'd be available to lend an ear if he ever needed one. As much as he appreciated her sympathy, he so didn't need to be viewed by anyone as some wounded soul who'd never gotten over past hurts.

Especially not by Hannah, of all people. After all, sympathy could all too easily turn to pity.

Because he *had* gotten over his past. He'd done quite well despite his past, in fact. That's what he preferred people to focus on. He was a successful businessman who'd grown from a hotel busboy to overall manager to hotelier to hospitality magnate, with an impressive cache of international resorts to his name. And he'd done it all before the age of thirty. That was the man he wanted to be perceived as. Not the confused, unwanted teenager who hadn't known where his next meal was coming from.

Now, as they walked to the other side of town to make their dinner reservations, he could only wish he'd handled the whole fiasco better.

The gentleman in the square most likely hadn't even been his old man. And so what if he had been? His father would have been just as much a stranger as some random tourist or local who may have looked like him.

Hannah pulled him out of his reverie by pausing all of a sudden in front of a bench. "That's the most interesting and unusual statue I've ever seen."

Alden looked up to realize they'd reached the famous landmark Istanbulians were particularly proud of. He'd been here so often the novelty had worn off.

"That's Tumbuli," he explained. "He was a beloved cat who roamed this part of the city. The shopkeepers made sure he was well fed and taken care of. He liked to hang out on that particular bench. He lived a long life for a cat. But when the time came, the locals were so sad when he passed they commissioned that statue in his honor to sit in his favorite spot."

Hannah clasped her hands together in delight. "It's fantastic. How right you were to say this city adores its felines. What does the name mean?"

Alden rubbed his jaw, trying his best to come up with a comparable term. He offered the only translation he could come up with. "I guess the best equivalent would be chunky. Like I said, he was well fed."

Hannah released a peal of laughter that had him grinning in response. "Chunky cat! And he has his own monument. How wonderful."

Alden shrugged. "I wasn't kidding about how much the Turks adore their cats."

Hannah stepped over and sat down next to the statue, reaching out her phone. "Please do me the honor of taking my photo with the infamous Tumbuli."

Alden stepped closer to oblige when a smiling couple interrupted mid snap.

"*Lutfen*," the man said, motioning to the phone. "We can take you both."

Alden glanced at Hannah to gauge her reaction. She nodded enthusiastically. Handing the gentleman the phone, he sat next to her, the bronze cat statue between them.

He'd never before even thought to get a photo here. The story when he'd first heard it had amused him, of course. But he hadn't given it much thought since. Hannah's reaction was completely different.

The sheer joy on her face as their photos were taken bolstered his mood severalfold. It was hard to remain morose when she was around. The tense events of earlier were growing more and more distant. He should have never let his emotions get the better of him the way they had. He should have focused on the woman he'd been with and made sure to show her a good time.

Well, he was determined to do just that the rest of the night. This was a good start. He couldn't believe he'd forgotten about Tumbuli. He offered a silent thanks to the lost cat for the way he'd served to further lighten the mood.

The man handed the phone back and Alden thanked the both of them.

Hannah scrolled through the scenes. "I can't wait to send these to my mom," she said, the smile on her face not having wilted the slightest. "She'll get a huge kick out of the story behind the statue."

She'd have many more photos to send before the trip was over. A few more probably from tonight, he had no doubt.

Alden led her to the door of the restaurant and they were shown to their table. A server immediately appeared to fill their water glasses. She introduced herself as Fatima. Hannah beamed at the other woman's remarks while telling her about the purchases she'd made.

Alden took a sip of his water and used the moment to study her. Dressed in a silky top with her hair falling about her shoulders, modest pearl earrings adorned her ears. The hazel green color of her eyes were accented by the soft lighting in the room. Her cheeks were blush with excitement, soft pink gloss glistened on her lips. Alden found his gaze hovering on her mouth. How had he not noticed when they were kids how lush and ruby red Hannah's lips were? Kissable.

The word came to his mind unbidden before he pushed it away. Thoughts like that could only lead to trouble. He had no business thinking about kissing Hannah. Once this trip was over, he couldn't even be sure of the next time he'd see her again.

"Alden?"

He looked up to find her staring at him inquisitively. The waitress had left their table without him even noticing. She'd clearly just asked him something and he hadn't even heard. Man, he had to stop drifting off.

"I'm not quite sure," he answered the question he hadn't even heard, hoping the response was general enough to cover his distracted state.

She blinked up at him in confusion. Clearly, he hadn't answered in a way that made sense.

"You're not sure what you usually order here?"

"Oh, the menu is preset. Unless you have a special request. I think you'll like it."

"I'm sure I will."

He was certain of it. Just as he was certain he had to make sure to avoid looking at her lips while she ate.

Easier said than done, a soft voice inside his head mocked.

The enticing aromas in the air as she stepped into the restaurant had Hannah realizing just how famished she was. Savory spices, grilled meats, and a sweet syrupy scent all mingled together under her nose and made her mouth water.

The room itself looked like it could be something out of a historical movie set in the Middle East. Thick velvet gold trimmed curtains in a deep burgundy red hung from the walls. The round tables were covered in ornate table-cloths. Brass genie lamps set in the center with glowing candles cast shadows about the room.

Her creative side immediately kicked into overdrive. She couldn't wait to get a chance to sketch out some ideas inspired by the rich colors and images around her.

Alden seemed much less affected by their surroundings. But then, he was used to such experiences, whereas all this was so new to her. And she had him to thank for exposing her to it. If she'd turned down his offer to be his pretend wife, she'd be back home in Boston right now polishing her résumé and updating all her professional profiles. Bored out of her mind.

She cast a glance at him now. His sky blue shirt combined with the soft lighting brought out the hints of steel gray in his eyes. He'd rolled his sleeves up again, making it hard not to focus on those arms she found so appealing.

Enough. Hadn't she decided earlier on the balcony that they worked better as friends? She had to keep that in mind for the remainder of this trip.

Fatima returned with a large bowl of salad and scooped out a hefty portion for each of them onto gold-colored plates. The fresh array of bite-sized cut vegetables along with the tangy scent of vinegar and zesty lemon set her stomach to grumbling. She dug right in as soon as Alden picked up his fork.

Before she knew it, a platter of assorted grilled meats arrived.

"You were so right," she told Alden between bites of food. "This meal is fantastic."

"There's more to this place than just the food," he answered.

Before she could ask what he meant by that, the lights dimmed drastically. A set of curtains she'd assumed were covering another wall drew open to reveal a low-level stage. Flame-lit towers stood on each corner. Fatima reappeared to clear the table with speedy efficiency just as a steady beat of drums sounded through the air. The beat was soon accompanied by a guitar melody. Hannah turned around to realize a three-man band had set up and were beginning to play.

She gasped in surprise and delight when she turned back as a figure appeared on the stage. A dark-haired woman with flowing curls wearing a long skirt and multiple scarves around her shoulders. She began moving her hips to the music and dancing about the stage in her bare feet. Small cymbals on her fingers followed the beat of the music as she danced.

"A belly dancer!"

Alden chuckled. "That's right. It's dinner and a show."

"This is so much more than I'd expected," she said, unable to tear her eyes off the talented woman who appeared to be double-jointed in all manner of limbs.

"What kind of hus—?" Alden stopped and

cleared his throat before continuing, "What kind of host would I be if I brought you all the way to Istanbul and didn't treat you to a belly dancing performance?"

Husband. He'd originally been about to say husband.

For one insane moment, Hannah felt the urge to pretend. To make believe that what he'd been about to say was the reality. That she was here accompanying her husband on a business trip as she maneuvered a career crossroads. That they really were man and wife.

Stop. She had to stop. Friends, that's all they were.

The first song came to an end and the dancer jumped off the stage for the second one. Dancing about the room, she earned cheers and applause as she went to each table one by one. Hannah found herself bouncing and swaying to the catchy music right in her chair.

The dancer reached their table just as the third song began. At Hannah's chair dancing, she flashed her a wide smile and held out her hands. The woman was asking her to stand up and join her! In front of all these people. Hannah's heart surged to her throat, horrified at the mere thought. She didn't know the first thing about how to belly dance.

"Come on," Alden urged next to her at the table. "Give it a try."

The belly dancer nodded her head, reached for her hand.

She immediately shook her head, hoping she was doing so politely. "No, there's no way," she said, hoping the woman understood enough English, though her actions had to be clear enough about her response.

"I think you'd be good at it," Alden said with a laugh.

"No. I don't think so. There is not a chance in this lifetime you're going to catch me attempting to belly dance."

Yet somehow, she was on her feet a moment later, doing her best to move her hips the way the belly dancer was showing her. She had no idea if she was even close to getting it right. Doubling over in laughter every few beats didn't help.

The other diners began to clap but Hannah barely heard the applause.

She only heard Alden's amused laugher echoing above the music.

"Something tells me I'll be feeling a few aches in my hips and back tomorrow morning."

Alden led Hannah out the door of the restaurant and to the sidewalk. The stroll back to their hotel would take a while, but he figured they could use the air and the exercise.

"Nah, you're a natural. You may have been a belly dancer in a previous life."

Hannah laughed before replying. "Somehow, I highly doubt that. I'm lucky I didn't fall right over when she had me do that last move. I'm sure everyone thought I looked ridiculous."

That was decidedly not true. Alden didn't dare tell her the thoughts he'd been having while he'd watched her with the dancer. How he'd had to look away from the way her hips were moving to the beat and the effects those movements were having on him. As it was, he'd have to fight hard to keep from reimagining it all whenever he closed his eyes.

Man, he had it bad. It might be time to acknowledge that. So that he could make sure to fight it with all he had. This fake marriage set up was confusing enough without him blurring the lines even further simply because he'd been turned on by watching his faux wife dancing.

An image popped into his head of her dancing that way yet again. Only this time, it was just the two of them. Alone in a dark room. Alden her only audience, Hannah moving that way just for him and no one else.

No. No. No.

There he went again. He had to get a hold

of himself or the next leg of this journey was going to be a torture of temptation. He owed it to Hannah to remain professional until this arrangement was completed.

She suddenly paused and turned to him. The lights of the Bosphorus twinkled behind her, framing her face.

"I really enjoyed myself tonight," she said. "Thank you for setting up such a fun evening."

"You don't have to thank me, Hannah. I enjoyed myself too." She had no idea how much. The only time he'd been at that restaurant before, he'd been a guest of a potential business partner. He'd barely paid any attention to the entertainment then. Now, it would be all he'd associate the place with after tonight.

By the time they got back to the hotel, he'd managed to convince himself that if he tried hard enough, those images of Hannah dancing might somehow be erased from his mind.

Though a cold shower probably couldn't hurt.

She was much too hyped up to sleep. So far this day had been a kaleidoscope of new experiences. Hannah felt as if she'd lived an entire year in the few short hours since they'd arrived in Istanbul. It might have been nice to perhaps talk about it all with her companion slash fake husband, but Alden had excused himself and jumped in the shower as soon as they'd returned to the suite.

After freshening up herself, she just couldn't bring herself to crawl into bed knowing without a doubt that sleep would elude her. Wrapping the thick terry bathrobe around herself, she stepped back out into the suite and turned the television on.

A quick surf of the channels offered two different soccer games, a news show of some sort, and a movie. Despite not understanding the language, Hannah found herself sucked into what she could make out of the storyline, which seemed to feature some kind of love triangle where the heroine was torn between a penniless farmer and wealthy landowner.

Looked like some dramas were the same the world over.

Alden's thick baritone startled her from behind suddenly. "What are you watching?"

With a jump, she clasped her hand to her chest. So engrossed in the movie, she hadn't even heard him approach. Looked like she wasn't the only one unable to sleep. She hadn't even bothered to turn the volume up much, not like she'd be able to understand the words, after all.

"Sorry," Alden said. "I didn't mean to sneak up on you."

"Not your fault," she answered. "I'm just unexpectedly invested in this poor woman's saga. I can't even guess who she's going to end up choosing."

Alden narrowed his eyes on the screen. "Huh."

"I just wish I understood more of what they're saying."

To her surprise, he walked around the couch to sit next to her. He'd apparently showered with some type of minty soap that tickled her nostrils and had her resisting the urge to inhale deeply of his skin. The warmth of his body as he sat down next to her sent a shiver up her spine. He wore loose-fitting gray sweatpants and a tight T-shirt that accented the contours of his chest and shoulders.

Hannah blinked and turned her focus back to the screen.

"I could try to translate," he said. "I've been here enough times that I might be able to catch a few phrases here and there."

Hannah wanted to jump at the offer. Aside from wanting to know the dialogue, it felt nice to have Alden here sitting next to her while they watched a movie together. "I don't want to keep you up," she said instead.

He shrugged, the motion making his upper

arm rub against her shoulder and sending electricity through her core. It would be so easy to lean into him, then indulge in that urge to take in his minty scent. What would his reaction be?

Hannah squeezed her eyes shut to ward off the tempting thoughts. Alden had made absolutely no moves to indicate that any such action on her part might be warranted. He'd been completely aloof and unaffected. As far as she could tell, this inconvenient attraction she felt was completely one-sided.

"Whoa," he said suddenly next to her. "Did you see that?"

She had not. She hadn't even been paying attention to the movie since he'd sat down, despite being so fully engrossed before he'd entered the room.

The truth was it was getting harder and harder to notice much else when Alden was near her.

At some point, once the movie ended but before they'd had a chance to turn the television off, she drifted off to sleep. When she opened her eyes again, the television was playing a game show.

And she was wrapped around a sleeping Alden, sprawled in his lap on the couch.

She moved off before he could awaken and quietly made her way out of the room.

* * *

Alden appeared to have showered and dressed by the time Hannah made her way back out to the common area. She found him scribbling over printouts with a steaming cup of Turkish coffee. If he had any recollection of the way they'd fallen asleep together, he gave no sign. Except that he hadn't quite made eye contact since she'd entered the room.

"Can I order you a cup?" he asked as she approached, his gaze still focused on the paperwork in front of him.

"No, thanks. As good as it smells, I'm going to pass." The brew really did smell heavenly, rich and robust. But her heart was still beating rather rapidly as a result of the position she'd found herself in upon awakening earlier.

"I'll just wrap up and we can head out, then," he told her. "I have one more stop I'd like to make in the city before we leave for the island."

The stop he referred to turned out to be for her benefit, Hannah realized an hour later when she found herself in yet another shop that took her breath away.

She had to resist the urge to throw her arms around him as soon as they stepped inside. Yards of colorful fabric lined the walls and lay draped over fixtures throughout the store. Silks, satins, velvet, lace, and everything in between. The creative part of her mind slipped into overdrive. Already she could picture numerous dresses and outfits, her mind reeling with possibilities.

"I've booked us a private appointment," Alden informed her. "Take all the time you need to pick out what you'd like."

He had no idea how difficult that was going to be. Every inch of material in here called to her on an artistic level.

"They'll ship whatever you pick out back to Massachusetts," Alden added.

A flood of emotion rushed through her core. The gesture was so unexpected, so thoughtful of him, she couldn't find the words to express how much she appreciated it.

"I don't know what to say." Surprising her with an elaborate dinner complete with a belly dance show was one thing, but this was a whole other level of thoughtfulness.

Alden simply smiled at her. Hannah made herself turn around and made a show of studying the closest ream of fabric before she could do something foolish. Like throw her arms around Alden's neck and kiss him until they were both gasping for air. The way she so desperately wanted.

CHAPTER TEN

THEIR SHORT TIME in Istanbul had come to a close all too quickly. Hannah threw her bag over her shoulder and took one last longing look at the view of the grand Hagia Sophia outside her window. She'd have to make sure to make her way back to this city. Maybe with her mom, though her mother didn't really like to travel. She especially wouldn't relish the idea of traveling quite this far. Maybe Hannah would come back with a girlfriend.

A lump of sadness settled in her chest that the trip next time wouldn't be with Alden. Awakening in his arms wasn't a memory she would soon forget. On second thought, perhaps it would be a better idea if she didn't return to Istanbul at all. The memories might be too much, longing for a life she couldn't have too bittersweet.

As if thoughts of her mother had conjured it, her phone vibrated in her pocket and sounded her mom's ringtone. As inconvenient as the timing was—Alden was waiting for her to take her down to the boat that would transport them to the private island off the Greek coast— knowing her mother, if Hannah didn't answer now, she would just keep calling until Hannah finally picked up.

"Hi, Mama. I can't talk long, I'm afraid."

Her mother didn't answer right away. When she finally did, her voice sounded hesitant and more than a little irritated.

"I woke up early to call you, Han," she said, using the nickname she'd used since Hannah was a toddler.

Alarm suddenly raced through her. "Are you all right?"

"Yes, yes, I'm fine," her mother answered. "I called to ask you what exactly it is you're doing."

Hannah plopped down onto the mattress behind her. "What do you mean, Mama?"

Her mother sighed before answering. "You said you were traveling on business. But that picture you sent me with the statue. Han, it doesn't look like a business trip. And why are you out so late with Alden? I thought he was there helping you with a new international business client."

Hannah swallowed down a curse. She should

have saved the picture for another time. She'd just been so enamored and excited to share her amusement with her mother that she'd emailed it as soon as they'd gotten back last night. Big mistake.

"We just grabbed a bite to eat together. That's all."

The truth was her mother had assumed quite a bit when Hannah had announced that she'd be traveling with her former schoolmate overseas on a business matter. Hannah had jumped at the convenience of not correcting Mama's assumptions. It was just easier that way. Just like it was easier not to go into too much detail about why Justin hadn't quite proposed yet. As far as her mother was concerned, Hannah was still gainfully employed and blissfully about to become engaged.

She didn't want to think of it as being dishonest with her mother. No, it was just a little fib to protect her parent from over-worrying, as she was so prone to doing. But now one innocent picture had somehow thwarted her efforts at keeping her mother calm and unbothered.

"I see," her mother answered, her voice shaky and unconvinced.

Hannah sighed, noting silently to avoid sharing any more photos with Mama until she was back in the States to explain things fully.

"I just worry about you," her mother added completely unnecessarily. If there was anything Hannah knew down to her toes, it was just how much her only parent worried about her.

"There's nothing to worry about, Mama," she reassured, hoping she sounded convincing. "I'm just taking in a few sights while I'm here. I can't wait to tell you about it all."

"That would be lovely. I didn't even realize you were branching out internationally."

She was indeed. Just not in the way her mother thought. One more thing to explain once she had the chance. The two of them were going to have to spend a long day together upon her return. Not something Hannah was really looking forward to, as much as she loved her mother.

By the time she disconnected the call, Mama sounded only slightly less concerned. But it was progress and Hannah would have to take it.

Right now, she had a boat to catch.

Dropping the phone back in her pants pocket, she swung the door open to find Alden there mid-knock.

"Sorry, I'm ready to go. Didn't mean to hold you up."

He tilted his head, studying her. "Everything okay? You look flushed."

The time and effort it took to reassure her

mother whenever she was riled up tended to have an exerting effect. Oftentimes, it was exhausting and draining. But in Mama's defense, Hannah was all she had. Her mother had worked hard and put every penny she'd made toward ensuring Hannah had a secure future with a solid education and steady career to fall back on. Hannah was lucky to have such a devoted parent. Look how little support Alden had grown up with in comparison. Hannah really had no business complaining.

"Everything's fine. We were just catching up. She says to tell you hello."

He smiled. "I remember your mother," Alden said, wordlessly taking her tote bag and slinging it over his shoulder as they made their way out the door and toward the elevator.

"Nice lady," he added while they waited for the elevator doors to open.

"Nice and high-strung," Hannah replied. The words were out before she'd intended them. Hannah hadn't meant to say that part out loud. Alden merely lifted an eyebrow. He stood staring at her a moment longer, as if waiting for her to explain and tell him more.

Maybe someday she would.

Alden wasn't often at a loss for words. But he had been back at the suite before they'd left the hotel. It was obvious the phone conversation Hannah had been having with her mother that he'd walked in on was a heavy one. He'd wanted to make her the same offer that she'd made him. To tell her that he was there to lend an ear if she ever wanted to talk. That he could very well see how being the only child of a single mother might have had its share of challenges.

But the words hadn't come. Now it was too late.

It hadn't helped that he'd awoken on the couch and remembered they'd fallen asleep there together. Wrapped in each other's arms. He hadn't noticed when Hannah left his side before morning. But he'd felt her absence as soon as he'd opened his eyes. Then later, the way she'd looked at him back at the fabric store would be seared in his memory for a long time to come.

"Our bags should already be loaded onto the yacht," he told her as their town car pulled up to Ataköy Marina and the driver came to a stop.

Hannah blinked at him. "Yacht?"

He nodded. "That's right."

Their driver had reached her door and pulled it open, yet Hannah made no move to exit the vehicle. She continued to stare at him.

"Something wrong?"

With a shake of her head, she reached for her bag. "No, nothing. I was just expecting to take a ferry or something."

He had to chuckle at that. "Not too many ferries make stops at private islands."

"Right. Of course. Guess I didn't give it much thought."

She gave him a tight smile as he reached her side and they made their way to the vessel. When they reached their boat, the captain was on the deck, waiting for them. Alden recognized the man from the last time he'd taken this trip. Ali was a seasoned sailor with years of experience and a friendly smile. He helped them aboard and led them down to the cabin where a server greeted them with aromatic moist towels. Within minutes, they were sailing steadily through the Bosporus toward the Aegean Sea.

Hannah hadn't really said much since they'd arrived at the marina. Was she remembering how they'd fallen asleep in each other's arms last night while watching a movie? Was she as confused as he was about how things were growing increasingly complicated between them? How so many lines were being blurred between pretense and reality? Between friendship and intimacy?

Or maybe she was just quiet because she was

tired and he was overthinking things. Perhaps she was just hungry.

"Breakfast will be served fairly soon," he told her, in case that last theory was accurate.

"That sounds lovely," she answered, barely glancing away from her view of the water out the glass wall of the cabin.

Turned out he was right. Less than fifteen minutes later, the same server appeared with a cart bearing several trays and two steaming carafes. She rolled the cart between them and lifted the silver covers off several trays to reveal an array of dishes. Fresh fruit, feta cheese drizzled with golden oil, a colorful tray of olives, and crispy toasted pita bread the size of dinner plates.

"It's a traditional mezze," he explained to Hannah once the staffer had left, just for want of something to say. He reached for an olive and popped it into his mouth.

"I didn't think I'd be hungry for breakfast after all the food at dinner last night," Hannah said. "But this spread looks amazing."

She helped herself to a plate of cheese and pita bread, while he poured them both steaming hot black tea from one of the carafes.

Despite her appreciative words about the spread, Hannah seemed to merely be picking at her food.

"Is something on your mind?" he asked, setting his own plate aside.

Hannah put down her fork, took a sip of her tea before answering. "I guess I feel a bit unprepared. I don't really know much about this impending business deal you're after. Or anything about your potential partner who'll be hosting us. I'm worried about playing my part well enough if I'm going in cold."

Playing a part. Alden winced internally at her description. But the truth was she had a point. They hadn't had much of a chance to discuss the particulars. Now was as good a time as any.

"We'll be meeting Emir and his wife, Amal, upon arriving at their private island. Emir is looking to build an all-inclusive resort catering to families, hoping to draw clientele from all over the world. The idea is to develop a family-oriented version of a club med resort. With offerings that will include everything from excursions to water sports to a play park. The idea is to appeal to those with young children and teenagers alike."

"Sounds fun," Hannah said, sticking her fork in a piece of melon.

"That's the idea. Fun vacations with lots to do. And luxurious accommodations to rest up in afterward."

"That's where you're hoping to come in," she provided, taking a tiny nibble of the melon and distracting his train of thought before he could rein it back.

The key was to keep his eyes off those tempting lips.

"That's right," he answered, making sure to focus on her eyes. Though it was just as easy to get lost in their depths. "Emir's looking for an experienced investor to help him build luxury lodgings. I'm one of three currently in the running."

She nodded. "I see. And that's why you needed a wife. Because he's looking to appeal to a family-oriented market, so he'd prefer to do business with other family men."

Alden swallowed the bite of pita he'd taken. "Not that Emir has come out and said as such. Let's just say I needed all the advantages I could get on my side. And then you and I somehow ended up married anyway, so I figured it might be fate."

"Kismet," she said, without missing a beat. "As the folks back in Istanbul might say."

"Exactly," he answered, pouring more tea for both of them. "Kismet."

She'd never been on a yacht before. And to think, her first time aboard one, and it was taking her to an exclusive private island. For the first time since she'd agreed to this plan, Hannah was beginning to have some real trepidation about exactly what she'd gotten herself into.

What *had* she gotten herself into?

How in the world was she going to pull this off? She suddenly felt disoriented and out of place. The food in front of her looked heavenly delicious and smelled even better. But she could hardly summon any kind of appetite. She wasn't used to being served breakfast aboard fancy luxury vessels. Whereas Alden was so natural in such an environment that he'd actually forgotten to even mention how they'd be traveling.

The way Alden led his life could aptly be described as on a grand scale. Private appointments at exclusive shops, traveling by private jet and yacht, making business deals on private islands. Hannah had to wonder if a regular existence like hers seemed too mundane for someone like him. Like her father. After all, hadn't that been why her dad left? He'd wanted more than the quaint little family who lived in a small town on the outskirts of metro Boston. So one day, he just up and left. To look for something more than what her mother and Hannah could give. Something more grand.

She watched Alden now as he finished off the last of his hot tea and poured himself another cup. He seemed so confident, so unbothered about what they were about to take on. While Hannah was a quivering mess inside. What if she couldn't pull this off? What if she made an error so bad that they were found out for the fraudsters that they were and he lost this deal?

To her surprise, she felt a set of strong hands wrap around hers and squeeze tight. She hadn't even noticed that Alden had moved over to sit next to her and taken both her hands in his.

"Hey, you're shaking. Are you a nervous sailor? Are you getting seasick."

She swallowed before she could say anything and Alden apparently took that as an answer.

"Jeez. I'm really sorry, Hannah. I should have thought to ask about that."

He looked uncertain and crestfallen, clearly beating himself up, thinking he'd been remiss about ensuring her comfort. Great, now she could add guilt to the mishmash of emotions churning through her center. There was an entire cornucopia to add that one to—anxiety, nervousness, among others. Oh, yeah, there was also that inconvenient attraction that she couldn't seem to squash no matter how hard she tried.

"I can go find one of the staffers, they might have something to help you with the motion sickness."

She was about to tell him not to bother when the world seemed to shift on its side. The whole yacht suddenly lurched sideways. One second she was sitting next to Alden on the sofa as he held her hands, the next she was sprawled over his lap.

Was it even possible to hit a wave while traveling along a strait? She wouldn't have thought so. And then she couldn't think at all. Alden's arms were suddenly around her, his face tilted close to hers. She felt his hot breath against her cheek, could smell the teasing scent of that now so familiar minty aftershave. The heat of his skin sent warmth over her own. Her breath caught as he leaned his face closer.

One thought echoed through her head, though she knew it was, oh, so wrong to be thinking it. Ever since they'd walked into the fabric store. No, even earlier when she'd awoken in his arms.

Kiss me.

She wanted it more than she wanted her next breath. She'd wanted to taste him since waking up in his arms all those days ago back in Vegas. Maybe even before then, when they'd been just kids in high school.

Alden had either read her mind or, heaven help her, maybe she'd actually voiced the words aloud. His eyes suddenly grew heavy and dark, his breath came out in gasps. Time stood still as his mouth finally found hers.

The taste of him sent a surge of pleasure through her body. His mouth was gentle yet firm, his breath hot. Now that he was finally kissing her, she realized just how much she'd craved his touch all this time. Untangling herself from his embrace in the early hours this morning had taken all the willpower she'd been able to pull from the depths of her soul. Now she wished she'd succumbed even then. For she'd only served to deny herself this inevitable pleasure. Why had she thought she could fight it?

The sound of footsteps reached her ears but she didn't care to try and determine where they might be coming from. All she cared about was the feel of Alden against her, the feel of his lips on hers.

Someone cleared their throat behind them.

She couldn't tell which one of them came to their senses first. The next instant she was off Alden's lap and he was standing to greet the man who'd entered the cabin. She felt his loss like a bucket of ice water. The taste of him still lingered on her lips.

If the captain had witnessed their entanglement, he was doing well to not show it.

"Ali, I was just about to come up and ask if everything was all right," Alden said, his back to her. Was it her imagination or was there the slightest tremble in the way he stood. Could he possibly have been as affected by their kiss as she was?

"We're fine up there. I came down to check on you two."

Alden spread his arms out. "We're fine. Just wondering what happened."

Ali shook his head in clear disgust. "Some fools in a speedboat not paying attention. We had to maneuver as fast as we could to avoid them."

"I see, I'm glad everyone above deck is all right." He motioned toward Hannah where she stood. "As you can see, we're okay down here as well."

"Glad to hear it," Ali said, his voice relieved.

"Thanks for checking on us," Alden added.

"It was a pretty close call."

She might say the same, Hannah thought, biting her lower lip as heat flooded over her skin. Who knew what that bone-melting kiss might have led to if Ali hadn't interrupted to check on them.

She had no doubt that if things had gone further, she would have been powerless to try and stop it. She wouldn't have even wanted to.

CHAPTER ELEVEN

HE'D BE HARD pressed to say what might have come over him. Hannah appeared shell-shocked. Well, he was a bit surprised himself. He'd kissed her. And she'd returned that kiss with whole-hearted abandon.

Only, that had been so much more than a kiss. The world had tilted on its axis when he'd had his mouth on hers. He couldn't deny that he'd imagined what she might taste like, what she would feel like in his arms. But his imagination hadn't done justice to the reality.

The staffer who'd served them breakfast appeared as soon as the captain left the cabin. Now, as the woman went about clearing their plates, darned if he could come up with any remote possibility of what he might say once they were alone again. One thing was certain—he wasn't going to apologize. He didn't regret kissing her. It was practically inevitable. That didn't mean he could let it happen again.

They were treading a thin line here between what was real and what wasn't. For both their sakes, he had to make sure they didn't fall on the wrong side of that line.

When the woman left a few moments later, Alden attempted what he hoped might be an acceptable way to broach the conversation.

"Hannah, listen. I didn't—"

Hannah held a hand up to stop him before he could go any further.

"Alden, that's not necessary. I think it's best if we just focus on what's ahead. Do our best to get through these next couple of days on the island and work to get you this deal."

Okay. Message received. Loud and clear. Hannah didn't want to talk about their kiss. Damned if he could come up with a counterpoint to argue about it.

"I'm going to go freshen up before we make landfall," she added a beat later.

Their conversation once she returned to the sitting area consisted of nothing more than small talk. But there was no denying the proverbial elephant in the room.

Finally, he felt the slowing of the ship and less than twenty minutes later they were within swimming distance of Emir and Amal's island home.

"It's much bigger than I imagined," Hannah

said, her eyes focused out the window. "And so very green."

"It's a lush Mediterranean landscape. With lots of sandy beach in a prime location. Within a speedboat ride to both Greek and Turkish coastal land and tourist attractions. You can't ask for a better location for a resort," he told her.

She turned to look at him. "You really want this deal to go through, don't you? Even more than I might have guessed."

"It would be a tremendous advancement of my holdings. A once-in-a-lifetime opportunity."

She nodded, her lips tightening. "Then let's go make sure it happens."

Ali appeared a moment later to escort them to the speedboat that would transport them the rest of the way to land. Amal and Emir were there to greet them when they arrived at the beach.

Alden reached for Hannah's hand to help her out of the boat to find that she was trembling. The poor woman was beyond nervous. A stab of guilt hit his chest that he was the reason for her discomfort. He leaned over inconspicuously to whisper in her ear. "It's okay. I'll be with you every step of the way."

The wide-eyed expression she shot him in

response was impossible to interpret. "They're warm, kindhearted, and genuinely friendly people," he added.

She simply nodded as he lifted her by the hips and onto land.

Amal approached Hannah immediately, her arms spread out wide. Hannah accepted the hug without hesitation.

"Welcome, dear," the older woman began while still embracing Hannah. "We're so happy you've come to visit us."

Emir meanwhile shook Alden's hand with enthusiasm. "Congratulations, my friend. Can't wait to meet your new bride. If my wife ever lets go of her," he added with an indulgent smile in Amal and Hannah's direction.

Aside from a fresh haircut, Emir didn't appear all that different from the last time Alden had seen him. Jet-black hair trimmed short and combed neatly, the man had a striking face with sharp features and dark soulful eyes. His wife could be described as a stunner by any parameter. With wavy dark hair that hung clear to her waist, thick gold bangles adorned both her arms. She wore a flowing yellow dress that reached her ankles.

"So lovely to meet you," she was telling Hannah now. "We were so thrilled to hear that

Alden here had gone and gotten married since we'd seen him."

She flashed her wide smile Alden's way. "You certainly surprised us, I must say."

If she only knew. He and Hannah had been pretty surprised as well.

"You'll have to tell us how it came about," Amal added.

Hannah's eyes grew wide with panic. Alden could guess what she was thinking, that they hadn't even gone over together exactly what they would say to the Bashars about their unexpected nuptials. He tried to convey a reassuring message with his eyes. They'd be fine if she just let him do most of the talking and followed his lead.

"Thanks so much for your hospitality in having us," Hannah addressed Amal first, then turned her eyes to Emir.

"You're quite welcome," Amal answered. "We're so glad to have you both." She crooked her arm into Hannah's and the two began walking. Alden and Emir followed behind.

"So tell me about yourself. I understand you two have known each other for years."

Hannah glanced over her shoulder at Alden for some kind of guidance. But Emir intervened first.

"Give them a chance to catch their breath,

hanim," he said, wagging a playful finger at his wife. "They only just got here."

Amal fake pouted. "Fine. We'll show you to your cabin to freshen up. Come find us at the main house whenever you're ready."

Alden's steps faltered at her words. It was his turn to feel apprehensive. Cabin? He usually stayed in a suite at the main house whenever he was here to visit.

He turned to Emir. "A cabin?"

Emir clasped him on the shoulder. "I wanted to surprise you, my friend. We've just had it built. A model cabin like those we'd like to build for the resort for guests who want a more private space apart from the central hotel. Right on the beach. You and your wife will be the first occupants."

"Uh… Alden?" Hannah looked about the freshly painted cabin that was to be her lodging for the next two days. Hers and Alden's. The quaint yet small cabin with only one bedroom. And only one bed.

"Hannah, I had no idea," Alden began immediately once Emir and Amal left after showing them the cabin. "Usually, I stay at the main house when I'm here. In a suite with two separate bedrooms like at the hotel."

"Well, now what? We can't very well tell them

we refuse to stay in here. How would we ever explain why?"

He thrust his hands through the hair at his crown. "We'll make the best of it. I can sleep on the couch."

Right. Like that was even feasible. The couch was barely more than a love seat. Alden would either have to sleep sitting up or with his legs dangling off one end.

Hannah glanced about the room. Under other circumstances, the little house would be a delightful space to stay in. Nestled in a shaded brush area off the beach, the cabin was decorated with bright pastel walls and an elaborately designed woven rug on the highly polished floor. A large Palladian window offered a stunning view of the crystal blue water and the gray shadow of other islands in the distance.

A look at Alden's face told her he was thinking along the same lines. If it weren't for that kiss, they might even be joking about their predicament right now, teasing each other about who should get which side of the bed. But a boundary had been crossed back on the yacht. And there was no turning back.

But she had to try.

She crossed her arms in front of her chest. "Look, we can be adults about this."

Alden tilted his head. "I'm listening."

She nodded. "We've already fallen asleep together twice. Once in Vegas, albeit we were out cold. And once again in Istanbul. This will be no different."

He merely quirked an eyebrow. Alden was thinking of exactly how this time would in fact be different. The kiss on the yacht had been an acknowledgment that there was a clear mutual attraction between them. What if they were tempted to act on that attraction again? Their surroundings were certainly romantic enough to lend to temptation. The cabin practically hummed with honeymoon destination vibes.

They'd just have to ignore that. Hannah continued, "As far as what happened back at the yacht, it was a momentary lapse in judgment. I think we should both try and forget it happened. I, for one, have already begun to do just that."

The other eyebrow followed the first one. "Well, first of all, ouch. Also, what makes you think I'm concerned about that at all?"

Hannah bit the inside of her cheek. What was that supposed to mean? That he wasn't concerned because he was certain he wouldn't be tempted to kiss her again? Or that it wouldn't be any kind of big deal if he did? Both options stung. She wasn't even going to pursue the possible answer to either of those questions. There was no point.

"In the meantime, we have another issue to contend with."

Alden crossed his arms in front of his chest. "As much as I'd like to tackle one potential disaster at a time, I guess I'll bite. What issue would that be?"

"You heard Amal. They want to hear all about how we tied the knot. What exactly are we going to tell them? We have to be in sync."

"We stick as close to the truth as possible. I'll do most of the talking and you just follow my lead. That way, we won't even be lying to them."

Hannah felt her jaw drop. How could he even say that? This whole thing was one big lie. Alden leaned over and gave her a reassuring squeeze of the shoulder. "It'll be all right, Hannah. Trust me."

"Okay, it's just..."

"What?"

"I don't know. I just wish all this weren't necessary. That we didn't have to deceive such decent people."

"We aren't really, sweetheart. We've technically only told them the truth."

Technically. As far as the endearment went, she was going to ignore that for now. He'd clearly thrown it out absentmindedly, without any kind of meaning or intention behind the word. Just like the last time he'd said it.

"And what of later?"

"What do you mean?"

She shrugged, trying to put into words the anxiety that had been plaguing her since boarding that yacht hours ago. "Once the ruse is over. How are we going to explain what happened? Why we broke up?"

His eyes softened with sympathy. "You really care what they think, don't you? Despite having just met them."

"I care what they'll think of you."

He stepped closer to her. That minty scent she found so appealing now mixed with the smell of sun and sand and fresh sea air. "Don't worry about that. I'll think of a way to explain to Emir and Amal that things just didn't work out between us. That we wanted different things. As much as we care for each other, it just wasn't meant to be."

Yet more blurring of the lines. Were they still talking in hypotheticals?

She nodded slowly. "It's going to be like fiction imitating real life, isn't it? My pretend husband will break up with me just like my real boyfriend did."

Hannah wanted to clamp her hand to her

mouth as soon as the words left her tongue. What an asinine thing to say. Her words made absolutely no sense. Alden wouldn't be leaving her. One couldn't leave someone they were never really with in the first place. They weren't even a genuine couple, for god's sake.

So why had she said it?

Alden reached for her then, took her hand gently in his, pulled her closer. A world of meaning swam in his eyes before he spoke. "Any man who would leave you is a fool, Hannah. One who never deserved you in the first place."

Alden's phone pinged in his pocket, breaking the heaviness in the air caused by what he'd just said to Hannah. Heavy or not, he'd spoken the absolute truth. He couldn't imagine being the man who'd had Hannah in his sights, had her committed enough to want to marry him, and then foolishly let her go.

Hannah released a deep breath before pulling her hand out of his. "Go ahead and check that," she told him.

He pulled his phone out of his pocket and wakened the screen. "It's from Emir. He wants to know if we're up for some water sports. Says to change into swimwear and meet them on the beach if we are."

Hannah peered over to take a look at his screen. "Huh, I wonder what he means."

An emoji popped up in the next second on his phone. An image of an airplane. Followed by yet another, this time a set of skis.

"Looks like he's asking us to Jet Ski."

"I've never been on a Jet Ski before."

"What do you say? You up for it?"

Alden willed her to say yes. He could certainly use the distraction. Not to mention, being alone with Hannah in such close quarters, in this charming romantically decorated cabin, was distracting him in ways he had to stem.

She gave him a tight smile. "Sure. Why not?"

Less than fifteen minutes later, they were exiting the cabin dressed in swimsuits and lathered up in sunscreen. Alden made sure not to notice the toned strip of tanned skin exposed between Hannah's tankini top and her boy short swim bottoms. She'd wrapped a long sheer scarf around her waist. Her hair was clipped in a high pile above her head. Cat-eye sunglasses lent an exotic accent to the overall outfit.

The woman certainly looked good in beachwear. He gave his head a shake. So not the time to be thinking that way. Yeah, he could definitely immerse himself in some cold refreshing water.

Emir and Amal were waiting for them down on the beach. A pair of water scooter Jet Skis were anchored several feet in the water.

"Just bought these," Emir said as they approached. "Plan on buying a fleet of them as an excursion option for guests. Thought the four of us could take them for a spin."

Alden didn't have to be asked twice. "Sounds fun. Let's do it."

Emir made his way to one of the machines, his wife trailing behind. Helping his wife onto the seat, he hopped on in front of her, Amal's legs cradling her husband's hips.

Alden turned to see Hannah swallowing, her lips tight. They'd be riding the same way.

"If you're not up for this, I can go for a spin by myself."

The other couple were waiting for them expectantly. Hannah shook her head. "No. I'd like to try. Looks like fun," she said, sounding much less enthusiastic than he'd felt when he said those same words moments ago.

He took her by the hand and led her to the empty Jet Ski. Helping her onto the seat, he took a deep breath before sitting down in front of her. The contact sent immediate jolts of electricity through his system. The seat wasn't very big. Hannah's legs wrapped securely around his thighs. Her arms curled around his waist.

Torture. Absolute torture.

Alden knew without a doubt that he'd be thinking about the feel of her inner thighs tight against him for the rest of today and well into the night.

And he'd be spending the night with her in a small secluded cabin. Heaven help him.

"Alden," he heard her say into his ear. "Emir's waiting for you to start the engine. Didn't you hear him?"

He'd be hard pressed to hear anything over the ringing in his ears. Alden turned to give Emir a thumbs-up, then turned the key and the Jet Ski came to life with a roar. The next instant, Emir had taken off and Alden followed suit. Hannah's arms tightened around his waist and another bolt of awareness speared through his chest.

Focus. He was operating a heavy machine for heaven's sake. Maneuvering it around water that was several feet deep. He had to get a grip and concentrate or they were both going to topple over.

In more ways than one.

In all her years on this earth, Hannah was pretty certain she'd never felt such a huge rush of adrenaline pour through her body. Alden was zigzagging around the water, the Jet Ski kicking up a spray that splashed all around them, thoroughly soaking her hair and skin.

It all felt tremendously exhilarating.

A flurry of sensations flooded her system. The cold of the water. The thrill of zipping through the waves. Hearing Amal's laughter over the loud roaring of the Jet Skis.

Oh, and there was also the exquisite feel of Alden's hard muscular waist and hips between her legs. That last sensation would have to be fought off with all her might.

"You still sitting securely back there?" Alden asked over his shoulder. "I can slow down if you want."

"Don't you dare. In fact, I think we should challenge those other two to a race."

Alden visibly did a double take at her answer. Well, she'd somewhat surprised herself. She was having fun! Pure and simple. Hannah couldn't recall the last time she'd enjoyed herself with such abandon.

Alden got Emir's attention and motioned for him to stop. When he did, he pulled up alongside the other couple and thrust his thumb back to motion to Hannah. "My lady here is challenging the two of you to a race."

Emir flashed a wide smile, his wife laughing and nodding enthusiastically behind him. "Challenge accepted," he answered, pointing to the distance at a large rock structure jutting out of the water. "First to the ocean rock wins."

"Hold on, babe," Alden threw behind him. Then he floored the Jet Ski the same instant Emir did.

She held him as tight as she could as they flew across the water. By the time they reached the rock, it was hard to tell who won. It was also hard to tell which of the four was laughing the hardest.

"Rematch at another time," Emir yelled over the roar of the engines.

"Just name the time," Alden said, his voiced laced with mirth.

Hannah got the distinct impression this was the beginning of a playful new rivalry. Alden would be here a lot if he got this deal. Judging by how competitive the two men seemed, she was certain the Jet Ski race was about to become a regular tradition when Alden was here.

Too bad she wouldn't be accompanying him.

"I have sea salt in all manner of places on my person," Hannah declared when they got to the cabin two hours later.

Alden tried hard not imagine where those places might be, but his imagination was inconveniently way ahead of him. They didn't make it back to the cabin until the Jet Skis had begun to run out of fuel and each of them had taken a turn driving. He might have to invest in one of those machines to keep at one of his beach-front properties back in the States. Hannah had gotten the hang of it in no time, maneuvering the vehicle over the waves. He'd invite her over to use one when they were home. Maybe on a long holiday weekend when he happened to be in town. Nothing said they couldn't hang out together once all this was over.

Right. As if their situation wasn't compli-cated enough without further entanglement after.

"You should have warned me about how salty the Aegean is." She wagged a finger at him.

"You shouldn't have spent so much time in the water." He reached for her hand after shut-ting the cabin door behind them. "You're prun-ing all over."

It wasn't wise to keep touching her. Even a gesture as innocent as holding her hand only led to thoughts of touching her in other ways.

Not good.

"I'll be a gentleman and let you have the shower first," he told her, letting go of her hand but not before his skin brushed against the ring on her finger.

He certainly didn't feel like a gentleman a few minutes later when he heard the water come on. Immediately the images flooded his mind. Images of Hannah under the steamy spray, lathering her bare skin, the bubbles cascading down those crevices she'd mentioned having salt in earlier.

Alden bit out a silent curse. At this rate, he wasn't going to need any hot water once he got in there to shower. When she emerged from the bathroom ten minutes later wrapped in a thick Turkish towel with her wet hair twisted atop her head, Alden gave himself an imaginary pat on the back for looking away and not letting his gaze linger.

"It's all yours. I'm not sure how much hot water I left you though."

If she only knew how little he needed it. "You'll have to find a way to make it up to me, then."

Now why had he gone and said something like that of all things? Full of innuendo. Hardly appropriate. Hopefully, Hannah wouldn't take it that way. He quickly veered the conversation back to the more mundane. "You have some time to rest. We're not due to meet Emir and Amal for dinner for another three hours or so. They eat pretty late in this part of the world."

She gave him a tight smile. "Guess I'll go take advantage of some downtime before I get dressed, then." She shifted the towel higher above her chest. "I thought I saw a robe hanging off the wall in there."

Great. Now he would have the pleasure of picturing her lying down in the other room on the bed with nothing but a robe on. Well, he shouldn't be picturing her in anything. Wait... that wasn't quite right either.

Alden blew out a breath and made his way to the bathroom. One thing was certain, feeling Hannah's legs cradled around him on the water had kicked his libido into high gear. Which was absolutely unacceptable. He had to stay sharp while they were on the island. With his eye strictly on the prize they'd come here for. To get that contract signed and move forward with this deal. Whatever was happening between him and Hannah would have to be addressed at some point. But this was not the time. Marriage certificate or not, they weren't here on this island to play some pretend version of house. They were here on business. Meanwhile, he would have to learn to keep his inconvenient yearnings in check.

He repeated that mantra in his head as he made his way to the bathroom and stepped into the shower, and then several more times as he bathed. The cleansing water did wonders to clear his head. See, he could be a rational and sound man when it came to his quote/unquote wife. By the time he wrapped the large towel around his middle, he was convinced.

Hannah was still in the bedroom with the door closed when he finished. Which posed a small problem. All his clothes were in the closet in there.

Lifting his hand to knock, Alden stopped when he heard the sound of her voice behind the door. She was talking to someone. Had Amal shown up while he was showering? But that made no sense, the two of them would be sitting out here to chat. Not behind a closed door. Plus, Hannah's was the only voice he heard. She must be on the phone.

Alden waited outside the door, not wanting to interrupt. Hannah's voice sounded tight and strained. Maybe she was talking to Justin. A spike of emotion he didn't want to name speared his chest, a cross between irritation and anger. If her ex was upsetting her, he had half a mind to barge in there and grab the phone to give him a piece of his mind. That man was out of her life for good now. The sooner Justin realized it, the better.

Only, what if he wasn't? What if he was working to reconcile their relationship? What if he'd come to his senses and realized how asinine he'd been to let Hannah go?

The feeling in his chest expanded, turning

into a gnawing ache he'd have been hard pressed
to describe.

Deep in thought, he didn't even notice when
Hannah stopped talking. An instant later, the
door swung open and she barreled through it.
Straight into his chest.

His towel wasn't going to hold.

CHAPTER TWELVE

SHE'D SOMEHOW JUST walked into a brick wall. Only the wall, though solid and hard, was made of flesh and muscle.

Alden was the wall.

And he was practically naked. Aside from a towel that he was hanging onto for dear life with one hand as he used the other to stay Hannah. To no avail, as she'd landed square against him.

"Oh, my God," Hannah blurted, covering her eyes in case the towel struggle didn't go Alden's way. But not before she got a glimpse of a set of hard toned abs glistening with moisture from his shower. "Could you please get dressed?"

"I'm sorry," Alden said, his voice reverberating around the cabin. "That's what I was going in there to do."

Okay. There was no need for panic. They weren't a couple of hormonal teenagers. Not anymore. Just because Alden's body was snug up against hers without any clothes, and the fact that she was also naked under this robe, wasn't cause for any hysteria. Squeezing her eyes even tighter and sucking in a breath, Hannah stepped to the side.

"By all means. The room is all yours. I'm sorry to have stayed in there so long."

Alden didn't move. What was he waiting for? "There's no need to apologize. And you can open your eyes, Hannah. Towel crisis averted."

He was so wrong about that. Because her fingers itched to trail a path along those abs she'd caught a glimpse of. To rip the towel off him herself. Pity that he'd been able to catch it in time before gravity could have done it for her.

Just. Stop.

She lifted one eyelid and then the other. Alden cleared his throat. Still hesitating. Hannah took a small step back for some distance but still Alden made no move. The air around them grew charged and thick. The sound of heavy breathing echoed through the small space. She couldn't even tell if it was coming from her or Alden. Maybe it was both of them.

Finally, Alden cleared his throat. "I'll just go grab some clothing, then."

Stepping around her, he closed the door softly behind him. Hannah stared at the dark wood panel. What might have happened just then if she'd lowered her guard for even a split second? Would she be in his arms right now? No towel? No robe? Would his lips be on hers? Hannah lifted her fingers to her mouth, recalling the sensations from the way he'd kissed her back on the yacht.

She'd been so distracted after her phone call that it was a wonder she'd managed to keep her wits about her just now when they'd been skin to skin. For a moment, when Alden hadn't moved, she'd been certain he was about to kiss her again. Probably just wishful thinking on her part. He'd simply stepped around her to go get dressed while she'd stood there like a quivering mess at the contact.

As for the kiss before they'd landed on the island, she'd been the one to initiate it, hadn't she? The fact that he hadn't pushed her away meant absolutely nothing. He practically apologized for it afterward.

She had to get a grip. Alden was here for a business deal. Their marriage a simple convenience that would be rectified soon enough.

But it was hard not to imagine those hard sharp-cut abs under the waistline of the khaki shorts he wore when he emerged from the bedroom a few minutes later. A round rim collared blue-gray shirt matched the color of his eyes.

He smiled at her. "Emir mentioned we'd be eating outside. Casual beach attire should work."

Was he hinting that she should get dressed? They still had at least two hours before they had to meet the other couple. In her defense, she'd pulled her dress out of the closet to throw it on before her mom's phone call had distracted her.

"I didn't mean to rush out and ram into you just now." She motioned in his general direction. "Impressive reflexes."

He nodded. "Yeah, that could have gone a whole other way."

He rammed his fingers through his hair, as if not quite content with the way he'd responded. For her part, Hannah wasn't sure how to respond in turn. Luckily, Alden changed the subject.

"You seemed pretty distracted. And I couldn't help but hear you talking to someone right before you came out."

So he'd heard her, then. Had he heard her try and stifle her sniffles? Could he guess that her throat was achy now from trying to hold back her emotions after talking to her mother?

Her expression must have given her away. "You wanna talk about it?" he asked. Alden was a pretty astute man. Funny, she'd said very much the same thing to him back in Istanbul.

She sucked in a fast breath and made her

way to the sofa before plopping herself down, rather ungracefully at that.

"My mom called again. She wasn't happy." *With me*, Hannah added silently. Mama made no secret of it when she was unhappy with Hannah.

Alden sat down on the other end of the sofa. "What happened? Is she all right? Didn't she have some kind of cardiac issue all those years ago?"

"Oh, she's fine. Her heart is monitored regularly at Mass General by one of the finest cardiologists in Boston. Physically, she's okay."

His eyes narrowed on her, listening intently. It surprised her that she did want to talk to him, to vent to someone willing to listen. She instinctively knew that Alden would do so without judgment or any attempt to advise. Unlike Justin. Who'd told her more than once that Hannah should simply declare her adulthood and brush it off whenever her mother was upset.

Justin had never understood just how much easier that was said than done, given the way she'd grown up.

"Justin stopped by the house to drop off some of my things," she told Alden. "Guess he wanted to get rid of what little I'd left at his place and didn't want to wait for me to return back to my apartment."

She thought she heard Alden utter a vicious curse before she continued. "I hadn't exactly given my mom all the details about what I'm doing here."

"Let me guess. Justin did the disservice of filling her in."

Hannah nodded in answer. "It's my fault really. I should have come clean before we left."

A flash of dark shuttered in his eyes before he spoke. "Why are you making excuses for him?"

She was doing no such thing. "I'm not," she said, more than slightly taken aback by the intensity in his voice. "I'm only saying that I shouldn't have put off the inevitable conversation I ended up having with my mom."

"What did you tell her?"

She sighed, recalling the long silences through her smartphone speaker as she waited, heart pounding for her mother to respond to each new revelation. "I said that we connected at Max and Mandy's wedding. And you mentioned a job opportunity that I'm here now exploring with you. But she pressed and pestered me with questions until I admitted that I'm considering a complete career change. Which she's not happy about." That was an understatement. "So she's now worried about not only my defunct relationship but also my stalled career. A career she worked about just as hard for as I did."

Alden reached for her hand, took it in his strong one. "I know she sacrificed a lot for you. It's only natural that you feel indebted."

Hannah bit the inside of her cheek. Not many people understood the bond between her and her mother. But Alden might understand better than most, given his background.

"All my life, I've only wanted her to be proud of me. Lately, all I've done is disappoint her."

He gave her hand a squeeze. "That can't be true. She has to be proud."

Hannah grunted a disbelieving response. "I don't know about that."

"How can she not be? You worked your way through school. Helped your mother out over the years. Look how accomplished and bright you are, with a head for numbers I could never hope for. And you have a creative side that you're not afraid to pursue. You're an amazing woman, Hannah."

Hannah swallowed; her mouth was having trouble working. Was that really how Alden saw her? The way he'd just described her had a lump forming in her throat. She couldn't seem to tear her gaze away from his.

"Thank you for that," she finally said when her tongue worked again.

"I'm only speaking the truth. Look how quickly Emir and Amal took a liking to you.

They can see what a special person you are. And it took them no time at all."

She was perilously close to giddiness. "You should stop now, before my ego grows to the size of that massive rock out there."

He laughed, moved his hand to entangle his fingers around hers. "It must have been hard for you and your mother. Being each other's sole source of familial and financial support."

She shrugged, trying desperately not to be too distracted by the way their fingers were linked together. "I still considered myself very fortunate. We didn't have much materialistically, but my mom was devoted and loving. I never felt alone." She gasped as soon as the words left her mouth. How thoughtless of her to say such a thing, given what Alden had dealt with. "I'm sorry. I didn't mean—"

He cut her off. "That's okay. It's the truth, after all. I was often alone."

Her curiosity piqued once again about something she'd always wondered since they'd been kids, and she had to ask. "How did you manage, Alden?"

He lifted one shoulder. "You know how. Worked odd jobs, ate at Max's often. Wore donated clothing." He said it all without a hint of embarrassment or self-pity in his tone, simply stating his truth.

"I don't mean financially. How did you manage without anyone there for you?"

The grip on her hand tightened for a second before loosening once more. "My dad wasn't really a warm father even before my mother left. I always felt like he was just going through the motions, you know? When it was just the two of us, he completely shut down. And then one day he just announced he was leaving to go back home to Cyprus. Wasn't sure when he'd be back." He grunted an ironic-sounding laugh. "I know now he had no intention of returning, was just playing me lip service."

Hannah's heart was shredding in her chest. Alden must have been so confused, felt so rejected. First his mother abandoning them, then his dad leaving. The two people who should have cared for and loved him more than anything else. Certainly more than themselves.

"He didn't ask you to go with him?"

Alden took a while to answer, staring at some vague spot between their legs on the sofa. "No. But I decided to try anyway."

"You did?"

A sad smile spread over his lips, without any hint of amusement whatsoever. "About a year and a half after he left. I scraped and saved, worked long hours on top of studying and football to save money for a plane ticket.

Max's father helped, told me it was a loan but I don't think he would have ever asked for the money back. Finally, after several months, I had enough to fly to Cyprus to visit my father."

Whatever memory Alden was recalling, it wasn't a happy one. He continued after a pause. "I told him I was coming, when I'd be there. Asked him to pick me up. I thought maybe I might even stay. Start a whole new life there with my dad."

She remembered hearing rumors during their sophomore year that Alden might move. Remembered how distraught she'd been that she wouldn't see his smiling face every day at school.

"What happened?" she asked.

The smile tightened. "Well, he hardly seemed thrilled to see me, first of all. Barely acknowledged me when I landed. Took me to his new house by the sea. By then he'd already begun a new family."

"Oh, Alden." He'd never spoken of it when he'd gotten back to the States. But everyone could tell there was something different about him back then. The ever-ready smile was just a little faded, the brightness of his personality slightly dimmed.

"New wife. New twins."

"So you decided to come back."

"There was no room for me there. I didn't fit in. Not in the country or village. And certainly not in my father's new house."

There were no words she could say, nothing to soothe the hurts he must be reliving. So she remained silent, letting him speak.

"However, like a fool, I still thought about maybe trying harder to fit in. Working around the house, helping with his acres of land."

She was afraid to ask what might have happened to change his mind. When he told her after a brief pause, the truth was so much worse than she might have imagined.

"One morning, I overheard his wife arguing with him, demanding to know when I'd be leaving. She'd grown tired of having me around."

Hannah swallowed, itching to wrap her arms around him. "I remember freezing where I stood, listening. Willing my father to stand up for me. For once in his life to choose me."

She could guess how that turned out.

"He didn't," Alden confirmed. "His response was to tell her that he'd figure out how to get rid of me as soon as he could."

"Oh, Alden," she repeated, at a complete loss for anything else to say.

"It gets better. He went on to say that he'd never even felt any connection between us. The way he felt with his new children. Not when I was born and certainly not later."

Oh, no. She couldn't even begin to imagine the wounds that must have caused, overhearing something so callous and cruel. She pictured a shocked and saddened teen boy, barely more than a child really, hearing his own parent being so cold, so uncaring. And so soon after being abandoned by his mother. She couldn't imagine the devastation such words might have caused.

Somehow, when Alden continued, his story only got worse.

"But he wasn't done appeasing his new wife. Who clearly wasn't thrilled that he'd had a family before meeting her."

"What else did he say?" she asked, afraid to hear the answer.

"He added that given my light eyes, and how different we were in disposition and personality, he had his doubts about me."

Hannah's heart pounded as she asked the next question. "What kind of doubts?"

Alden rubbed a hand down his face. "He said he couldn't be sure I was even his son."

Hannah couldn't help her gasp. If Alden's father were standing before her now, she'd gladly throttle him until the man turned purple. How despicable to say such a thing about your own flesh and blood—apart from his mother's eyes, there was no doubt Alden was his son.

Her mind was scrambling for a way to tell him he hadn't deserved such cruelty. No teenage boy did. But she didn't get a chance. Alden suddenly dropped her hand and stood. A curtain seemed to drop between them. He was clearly done sharing and the conversation was over.

"Why don't you get dressed and we can make our way over to the dinner spot a little early?" he suggested.

Okay. If he needed to move on from all that they'd just confided in each other, she would have to honor his wishes. What other choice did she have?

"Right. I'll just go throw a dress on and put my hair up."

"I'll wait here."

Hannah stood, threw him a friendly smile. "On the way there, you can tell me more about how special I am."

He chuckled, taking her hand once more and turning her palm over. The ring on her finger sparkled like a bright star in the rays of sunshine pouring through the window.

"Trust me. One day, the man that puts a ring on your finger for real is going to realize just how lucky he is."

Just like that, her attempt at humor came to a sudden, halting crash. Alden might see her as accomplished, bright, and attractive.

But ultimately, not for him.

CHAPTER THIRTEEN

A GENTLE BREEZE drifted off the sea and ruffled the wisps of hair around her face, bringing with it the scent of salt water and fresh sea air. They'd walked along the beach mostly in silence. Hannah couldn't imagine what she could possibly say as a response to the things Alden had told her back at the cabin. To think, all those years ago back in high school, he'd been carrying such a burden and hardly anyone, except for Max's family, had even known. They'd just pegged him as the independent teen who lived alone in that big house.

"Sorry if the conversation got a bit heavy back there. I want you to know, I don't really talk about those last couple of years of high school with anyone."

"I'm glad you told me. I still can't believe we had no idea about any of it when we were kids."

He thrust his hands into his pockets. "Max knew the overall gist of what was happening.

I just never told him the details. Actually, the part of the conversation I overhead, I haven't told anyone else but you about that."

That gave her pause. "Why not?"

Alden stopped walking, turned to face the direction of the water. Hannah followed suit and they both stared at the sun setting on the horizon in the distance. A kaleidoscope of bright oranges and shades of yellow layered the sky.

He'd been silent so long Hannah figured he wasn't going to bother answering her question. "It isn't exactly a fun story, right? The poor kid whose parents left him to head for greener pastures. Whose father didn't even want to claim him as his own son."

"Thank you," she said simply, meaning it with her whole heart. It meant more to her than Alden might have guessed that he'd trusted her enough to speak of such a private memory.

He humphed. "For what? Bringing down the mood after what was a fun, enjoyable afternoon Jet Skiing with new friends?"

She chose to ignore that. "Stunning view, isn't it?"

He turned to face her. "Absolutely beautiful." His eyes roamed her face as he stepped closer. The next moment, she felt his breath along her cheek as he leaned closer. With the barest of a touch, he brushed his lips softly to hers.

Hannah's breath caught, her heart hammered in her throat. Just the barest hint of a kiss. One might not even call it that. But she felt it clear to her toes, her skin tingling outward from her lips.

Until he leaned closer and whispered in her ear. "Hope that was okay. We have an audience."

Hannah turned to see Emir and Amal walking toward them in the distance. So the near-kiss was just for show, then. For the other couple's benefit. Alden may as well have doused her with a bucket of ice water. How horrifying.

Once again, she'd been ready to throw herself at him when Alden clearly had no such inclination. What in the world was wrong with her? Somehow, she managed to steady her pulse and paste a fake smile on her face in preparation for meeting the other two.

And if there was a subtle stinging behind her eyes... Well, no one needed to know that, did they?

Amal and Emir reached their side a moment later.

"We were just coming to get you," Amal said, putting her arm through Hannah's. "See if you were ready for dinner."

Another pang of guilt shot through her. Amal was so warm and friendly; she acted like they'd known each other for years as opposed to just a few hours. Hannah felt as if they were long-standing friends. It pained her that she wasn't being completely honest with such a genuinely decent person. Her husband too.

"I hope you're both hungry. Dinner's just been put out for us," Emir added. "We'll be eating outside by the water. This way."

The four of them started walking in the direction the other couple had come from. Soon, they approached a cabana tent with a round table in the center covered in a blue canvas cloth. Strings of tea lights hung along the rim of the top. Four place settings surrounded a round lazy Susan in the center. Alden guided her to one of the chairs and pulled it out for her. He took the seat immediately to her left while Emir did the same for his wife, then sat across Hannah.

Hannah lifted the silver cover in front of her to reveal a dish of grilled fish with a side of aromatic leeks dotted with gem-green scallions. A separate large bowl contained a generous helping of fresh vegetable salad with cucumbers, tomatoes, and herbs, and sprinkled with pomegranate seeds. A rounded circle of pita bread sat atop a quarter plate near the salad, steam drifting off the fresh dough.

"Today's catch," Amal remarked, lifting her own cover. "Fresh from the sea less than an hour ago. Just-caught fish tastes so different."

Hannah's mouth watered. Emir motioned for them to start and she did so with gusto. The food tasted even better than it looked. Amal hadn't been wrong about how fresh the fish was. The tender meat practically melted in her mouth. The vegetables and the salad tasted as if they'd just been picked off the vine. She suspected they must have been.

"Wow," Alden said next to her. "If this is the kind of food you plan on serving at the resort, I think we're going to have a very popular food destination here."

Right. She'd almost forgotten. This entire trip was all for ensuring Alden got his business deal. How silly of her to lose sight of that for even a moment. She felt for Alden, she really did. Her heart was still breaking over what he'd told her back at the cabin. He couldn't have had it easy, fending for himself after losing both parents. But this laser-sharp focus of his to achieve business success seemed almost excessive.

In many ways, that quality in him reminded her of the way she'd been brought up. No accomplishment on her part was ever enough. Mama was always focused on the next big achievement.

Apparently, so was Alden.

"So tell us," Emir said, pushing his now-empty plate away. "Last time Alden was here, he was an unattached bachelor. Then he shows up with a beautiful wife. How did that come about?"

Across the table, Hannah dropped her fork before Emir could even finish his question. It landed with a loud clanging onto her plate. She threw him a wide-eyed glance full of panic.

Alden shot her what he hoped was a reassuring smile. Did she honestly think he hadn't been prepared for such a question?

"Hannah and I have known each other for decades," he answered, dabbing his mouth with the cloth napkin, then setting it on the table in front of him. "We lost touch but as soon as we saw each other again at mutual friends' wedding, the sparks immediately began to fly. For me, anyway."

Now why had he admitted that last part? More importantly, was there any truth to it? He gave himself a mental head shake. Of course there wasn't. He just had a "type" he was attracted to, that's all.

Hannah sat staring at him with her mouth

agape. He'd have to answer some questions later about that last statement, no doubt. But it wasn't as if he could pull the words back. "I guess I've always had a crush on her," he added, figuring that if he was in for a penny, he may as well be in for a pound.

Amal gave a delighted clap. "That's so romantic. Lost love that was found again. So many years later."

"Something like that," Hannah answered. Her cheeks were flaming red, her head ducked with eyes averted downward. He really owed her a world of gratitude, given how uncomfortable she was with the farce.

"So then I had to admit that I'd had a crush on her all through school. And apparently I never got over it."

Hannah lifted her head, her eyes found his. "I've had a crush on him too," she said softly. "All this time."

Whoa. For someone who'd felt so disquieted about playacting, she sounded pretty convincing. Unless...

Emir didn't give him a chance to ponder on it. He clapped Alden on the back. "I know I've said it before, but congratulations." He turned to Hannah. "To you both."

"Thank you," they said in unison.

Hannah added, "And we can't thank you

enough for your hospitality. The island is paradise."

Emir removed his hand from Alden's shoulder and leaned his forearms on the table, addressing Hannah. Alden felt a momentary panic that he might be about to ask her something about their marriage she didn't have a clear answer for. He prepped himself to intervene. But Emir threw him a curve ball with the direction he took the conversation.

"I understand you're a corporate accountant."

Hannah swallowed. "That's right. Though I'm at a bit of a career impasse right now."

Emir rubbed his jaw. "Oh, that's too bad. I thought maybe you could help us with the books once the resort opens. Seeing as your husband will be a partner investor."

Wait. Had he heard the man right? Hannah did a double take, blinking across the table at Emir. So she'd heard it too.

Amal confirmed a moment later. She gave her husband a playful shove on his shoulder. "Emir, you're terrible to try and tease them so. Just tell them you've made your decision and will accept Alden's offer."

Emir winked at his wife playfully before turning to Alden and extending his hand. Alden shook it with enthusiasm, then gripped the table edge tight to refrain from pumping his fist in the air. Finally. After all this time, and all the effort, he'd achieved success. He could practically taste the victory.

He owed a large portion of that victory to Hannah. He might never have gotten this deal if she hadn't accompanied him on this trip as his wife. And the way she'd charmed both Amal and Emir had no doubt helped immensely.

"I'm so glad we'll be seeing more of you two," Amal said, directing the words to Hannah. "This island was a wonderful place to bring up our children, you know."

Emir laughed out loud, then wagged a finger at his wife. "What a sly way to ask them about having children."

Amal's expression was full of chagrin. "My husband's right. That was much too personal. I'm sorry."

"Don't be," Hannah immediately responded, patting the other woman's hand on the table. "It's quite all right."

"Thank you. It's just that I have four children, all adults now but they're still babes in my eyes. All at university in the States."

"You must be so proud of them." Hannah said.

"I am. Family means so much. I miss them terribly. The house is so empty without them. I miss all the noise that comes with having a large family about."

"I would love a large family," Hannah said, her voice low and tender. "Someday," she added on a sigh.

A small ache twinged in Alden's gut. If he needed any kind of sign that he and Hannah were on different life paths, there couldn't be a much clearer one. As far as he was concerned, family wasn't in his cards. Why would he even make an attempt at such a life, given the way his own childhood had gone? He didn't know the first thing about being a decent father. Or husband for that matter.

It wasn't as if he'd been given any kind of decent example by his own parents.

Hannah deserved so much better than him. She deserved the family she wanted. She deserved stability. She deserved someone who knew how to love and be loved. Who knew what it felt like to be part of a family.

None of which could describe Alden Hamid. He couldn't give her any of that. Not even if he wanted to.

He couldn't imagine a reality where he would.

CHAPTER FOURTEEN

FOR A MAN who'd just won what he'd referred to as a deal of a lifetime, Alden appeared pretty morose as they made their way back to the cabin. After enjoying a dessert of sticky baklava at the main house, Emir and Amal had bid them good-night with the latter promising to send Hannah her secret recipe for the traditional delicacy.

Alden didn't say much during the walk. And he was just as quiet when they reached the door and made their way in.

"I thought you'd be in more of a celebratory mood," Hannah remarked, grabbing a bottle of water from the refrigerator and taking a long swallow. "There appears to be a bottle of something bubbly in there if you want to toast to your victory."

"Not for me. I guess I'm just tired."

Huh. In all the years she'd known Alden and the amount of time she'd spent with him since

Vegas, she'd never seen him exhibit any kind of exhaustion. On the contrary, he was high energy and constantly on the go unless he was asleep.

Her phone pinged in her pocket with an alert. For a second, she had a moment of dread at the thought that her mom might be calling or texting. Then a wave of guilt washed over her for having such thoughts about her own mother. She checked the screen to see it was just Amal.

"She's texted me a copy of her recipe card already for the baklava. I can't wait to try and make it back home."

Alden merely nodded, clearly feigning an interest he didn't feel. "I'm sure you'll do a great job," he said.

Maybe it was the scrumptious dinner, or maybe it was the fact that Alden's deal had finally gone through. Or perhaps it was all the talk about family back at dinner. But she decided to take a chance.

"Open invitation to come to Boston and have a piece when I try out the recipe. You have offices in the seaport district." She hated that her voice was shaky. Hell, her entire body was shaking. As casual as she was trying to make it sound, there was a lot riding on how Alden would answer.

He rubbed a hand down his face. That didn't

seem like a positive sign. She was right. "I don't think that's a good idea, Hannah."

She knew she should drop it. Just let the matter go. Everything about Alden's demeanor and his voice flashed a bright yellow caution sign.

Too bad she didn't heed the warning. "What about around the holidays then in a couple of months? Christmas in Boston is always a spectacle to behold. The tree at the Common is enough to make the trip worthwhile."

He shook his head slowly, his eyes holding steady onto hers. "I won't be in New England over the holidays. In fact, I'll probably have to spend those months back here to get started with the resort grounds breaking."

Then invite me along.

Hannah wanted desperately to say the words out loud. That little devil was back on her shoulder and urging her to do just that. But the yellow warning had turned to bright red.

"I see. I hope it all goes well, then." She took another swig of water and set the sweaty bottle on the counter between them, none too gently. "I'll see you in the morning. I'm going to bed."

He was around the counter and had reached her in less than three strides. He took her gently by the arm and turned her to face him.

"It would make no sense for me to visit you in Boston, Hannah. Not for either of us."

She pulled her arm free and crossed them both over her chest. "Right. Now that you've gotten what you wanted. You're forgetting something though, aren't you?"

"What's that?"

"The fact that we're still legally married. Small detail."

Something flashed behind his eyes that had her heart splitting in two. She wanted to walk away with her ears covered to avoid hearing what came next.

"I emailed my attorneys earlier. Right before dessert. Directing them to draw up the paperwork required for dissolution of marriage in Nevada. We'll just sign our names and it will be like the marriage never happened."

Her mouth went dry. The coldness of his delivery shook her to her center. He hadn't even waited a full hour after he'd gotten Emir's acceptance to set the divorce in motion.

"So that's it, then? All loose threads will be neatly tied. You'll have your business milestone. And you'll be rid of the wife you never intended to have."

And where did that leave her? She had no job, no prospects unless she begged to reclaim a position she no longer felt fulfilled in. To top it off, now she'd be nursing a broken heart.

"Hannah, it's not like that."

"Then please explain exactly what it's like." She held her palms up, waiting for what he could possibly say to make any of this better in even the most minuscule way.

"I know I owe you a large debt of gratitude. I've already started the process of having extra funds delivered to your bank account. There should be enough there to give you ample time to decide how you want to proceed about your professional future. I hope you follow your passion. I wasn't kidding when I said you had the talent to really make something of it."

Hannah's mind recalled all those scenes from classic movies where the starlet swung her hand back to deliver a well-deserved slap on the face of the man she'd fallen for, her love neither appreciated nor reciprocated. Her fingers itched with the desire to do just that. But she was no starlet. And this wasn't some romantic foreign movie like the one they'd watched together back at the hotel. Plus, if she were being truthful, she would have to admit that it wasn't anger she felt clear through her cells.

It was hurt. She'd fallen for Alden. Hard and deep. Hell, she might have always been in love with him. Since they were both teens.

While he still only saw her as a means to an end that he'd now finally achieved. Despite the time they'd spent together and all they'd experienced since mistakenly tying the knot back in Vegas, it hadn't affected him in any way. Unlike for her.

And now he was sending her away with nothing but a payoff.

Alden watched the light go out under the doorway of the bedroom. Hannah had gone to bed. He wouldn't bother her. He would stay out here on the sofa and let her get some rest. It wasn't as if he'd be getting any sleep anyway.

How had such a simple plan become so convoluted?

Hannah's invitation to visit her in Boston was so tempting on the surface. But he knew he'd be doing both of them a disservice if he took her up on it. He was too broken. Too damaged.

He had to disillusion her of any notion that he might be good for her. Hannah's future was too bright for him to dim it.

He stayed awake for hours, simply watching the sky outside grow darker until it finally began to lighten once more. The sun eventually appeared, flashing brilliant colors through the large window.

Eventually he must have closed his eyes. Because when he opened them again, the day had grown brighter. Thick puffy clouds dotted the sky above the water.

Someone had thrown a knit blanket over him at some point. Hannah. Even after the way he'd treated her, the thoughtless things he'd said, she'd cared enough to make sure he was warm during the night.

Glancing behind him, he realized the bed was made and the door was open. The room empty. Where was she?

Alden pulled his phone out of his pocket. It was already 11:00 a.m. Something else appeared on the screen. An email from Hannah.

He clicked it open and began to read.

Alden,
I've taken Amal up on her offer to travel to the mainland with her as she picks up supplies. I won't be returning when she comes back, giving her the excuse that I'd like to do more sightseeing in Istanbul while waiting for you. I've already said my goodbyes to both her and Emir.

I think it's best if I return home. Alone.

Congratulations. I'm glad things worked out the way you hoped.

Alden read it again. And once more. He kept reading until his eyes started to water, as if each pass through would reveal some hidden message that he'd somehow missed. Anything to make this awfulness feel better somehow.

She hadn't bothered to say goodbye to him in person. Not that he could blame her. It was no less than what he deserved.

With a silent curse, he tossed his phone away in frustration. Only he used too much force and wasn't surprised when it bounced off the coffee table and landed with a loud thud on the hardwood floor. A webbed array of cracks appeared immediately on the screen.

Something else on the coffee table caught his attention. A flash of brilliance flashed in his eyes as the rays of light from the sun landed onto the surface after a passing cloud. She'd left the ring behind.

Alden swore again and rubbed a hand down his face. The way they'd left things between them didn't sit right. A brick sat in the center of his stomach as he recalled the way she'd walked away from him before going to bed, the deep shadow of hurt behind her eyes.

He stood and reached for his phone. He had to at least try and call her, to try and explain. But even though the damaged device functioned enough to pull up the number and dial, the call went immediately to voice mail.

Hannah was gone. The only hint she'd ever even been here was the ring she'd left behind and her last message still on the screen of his damaged phone.

It wasn't the only thing he'd broken so carelessly.

Maybe she'd taken the cowardly way out, leaving before Alden had awakened. But there really was nothing left to say to each other. He'd gotten what he'd brought her here for.

And if she were being truthful, she had to admit that he'd never misled her. Never pretended that this trip was anything more than a business venture.

It was her foolish heart that had betrayed her. Falling in love with a man who didn't feel for her the way she felt for him.

Hannah paced the boarding area at Istanbul International Airport, willing for her row to be called. The sooner she got on that plane and made it back to Boston, the sooner she could begin to put the pieces of her suddenly disordered life together.

All while nursing a broken heart.

"You look like you could use a cup of strong Turkish coffee, my friend."

Emir stood up from behind his desk, closing the cover of the tablet he'd been studying. They were supposed to go over initial plans and blueprints but Alden had no idea how he might begin to focus.

"I had something of a restless night."

Emir studied him with alarm. "Did you not sleep well? Is something wrong with the bed at the cabin?"

Alden shook his head. Not that he would really know. He hadn't spent so much as a minute on the mattress. He opened his mouth to assure Emir that the bed was more than adequate, that it was as comfortable as the beds he'd slept in at five-star hotels. He stopped short before the words left his tongue. In the overall scheme of things, it was a fairly small fib. But Alden just couldn't do it. Suddenly, it was all too much. The false premise under which he and Hannah had arrived, the small untruths that were nevertheless misleading—it all weighed like bricks strapped to his shoulders.

Even lying about a simple mattress seemed just one more step in a vicious cycle that no longer seemed worth it. Alden didn't even care anymore about signing the contract with Emir. He would be disappointed to have it fall through. But there would be other business opportunities.

There'd never be another woman like Hannah. And he'd blown it with her. The way he'd acted, she likely wouldn't even consent to remaining his friend. She had every right to feel that way.

"Something on your mind?"

Alden looked up to find Emir staring at him, his head tilted in concern. There was no way he was going to continue with the ruse. Funny how much of a difference just a few short hours made with regard to what he'd thought were his top priorities. So many ill-thought-out decisions had brought him to this humbling moment.

Well, he'd just decided that he was going to stop lying to his friend. No matter what it cost him, he was ready to admit the truth. Without giving himself a chance to think and change his mind, he found himself blurting out the whole truth. Beginning with waking up married to Hannah in Vegas all the way to the horrible scene from last night and all the relevant details in between.

"I can only say I'm deeply, sincerely sorry," he finally finished, short of breath from all the talking.

Emir regarded him with eyebrows creased. Several moments passed without either one speaking a word. Finally, the other man cleared his throat.

"I thought my English was pretty good. But maybe not?"

Alden blinked at the comment. What did Emir's fluency have to do with anything? "Your English is excellent." He'd studied in the States, did business in Manhattan and Los Angeles regularly and several spots in between. So where was he going with such a statement?

"Then I'm wondering why I'm confused." He crossed his arms in front of his chest. "Let me ask you something. You and Hannah are married as of this moment. Correct?"

Alden could only nod.

"Hmm. I see."

"But we didn't plan—"

Emir held a hand up to stop him. "Please, just bear with me while I ask my questions."

Alden figured that was the least he could do. "Go ahead."

"It appears you and your wife had some type of argument last night. Is that correct?"

That would be putting it pretty mildly. And he really shouldn't refer to Hannah as his wife any longer but, on the surface, Emir was right, he supposed. "You could say that, yes."

"And you are an intelligent man. I know that or I would have never agreed to go into business with you."

Alden rubbed a palm down his face. "Uh… thanks, I guess."

"So please explain something to me then."

"What's that?"

"Why exactly are you here apologizing to me?"

Well, when he put it that way…

Alden blew out a breath. "Doesn't it bother you in the least that you were being lied to?"

Emir shook his head, gave him an expression that implied he might be second-guessing his estimation of Alden as a smart man. "My friend, I think you have been lying to no one but yourself."

His mangled mess of a phone began to ring just as Alden entered the cabin twenty minutes later. His heart leaped in his chest before he yanked it out of his pocket and glanced at the screen.

It was Max calling. Not Hannah.

Alden debated answering, his thoughts too jumbled to hold any kind of conversation at the moment. But then loyalty to his friend won out. What if there was some kind of emergency? He clicked on the call.

Max didn't wait for him to say hello. "And how is my only remaining bachelor friend?" he asked as soon as soon as Alden picked up.

Alden bit out a curse at the question. If Max only knew.

So, no emergency then. "Did you really call

just to ask me that?" he asked, hoping he didn't sound short given the way he was feeling at the moment. "On your honeymoon, no less?"

Max's laughter rang through the tiny speaker. "Of course not. I called because—" He paused to clear his throat. Then he cleared it again. Several moments passed by in silence. Alden glanced at the screen to make sure the call hadn't dropped.

When Max spoke again, his voice was thick and rumbled. "I just had a quick moment and wanted to call because—" His friend paused yet again. Was he actually getting emotionally choked up for some reason?

"What is it, man?" Alden asked. Maybe he'd been wrong about the emergency, after all.

"I just wanted to thank you," Max finally spit out. "For talking me down back in Vegas. I would have never forgiven myself if I'd left Mandy at the altar."

Alden sighed and plopped himself on the couch, the phone still to his ear. So that's what this was about. As much as he appreciated it, he had other things on his mind at the moment. Like his own fiasco around chaotic nuptials.

"Don't mention it, Max," Alden answered. "You just needed a little nudge in the right direction."

"And you were there to give it to me. Like

a true brother. Which is what you are, Alden. I mean that. You're just as much my family as my blood brothers."

The statement gave Alden pause. *Brother. Family.*

The realization hit him like a ton of bricks. All this time he'd been going about his days convinced he wasn't part of a family. When in fact he had been all along. Max was his family. All the Hartfords were. So was Mandy.

And so was Hannah.

He couldn't even recall when he'd lost sight of that truth. He'd convinced himself he wasn't cut out for such relationships. That he didn't want for any kind of family. Such a lie. When had he convinced himself of that fallacy? For the life of him, he didn't know. It was just as if gradually his fear had overcome his desire for connection the longer he was alone.

Except that he never really had been alone, after all.

He'd been such a fool. And he had to find Hannah to tell her just how foolish he'd been. Then beg her to love him anyway.

If someone had told him a month ago he'd be wandering the streets of Istanbul looking for his wife so he could return her wedding ring, Alden would have wondered which one of them might have lost their mind. But three hours after leaving Emir's office, Alden was doing exactly that.

With no luck.

He'd made his way to all the places they'd visited while in the city together. No sign of her. Now he was at the last place he could think of. Alden sat down on the bench next to the statue of Tumbuli and stared absentmindedly at the novelty shop across the street. The display window had an elaborate array of evil eye charms in varying sizes and colors. One was the size of a dinner plate surprisingly. Hannah might have gotten a kick out of seeing those.

She wasn't here either. Which left one very likely possibility—Hannah was currently already in flight. On her way back to the States. She'd left before he'd had a chance to even try and make amends.

He had no one but himself to blame. He wasn't sure how long he sat there when a small mewing sound reached his ears. Alden blinked and gave his head a brisk shake. Was that a meow he was hearing?

Okay. Clearly, he really had lost his mind because he was imagining a bronze cat statue was actually making cat noises.

Something soft and fluffy brushed against his ankle. He looked down to find a mound of fur moving over his foot. Leaning down, he picked it up. A small pink tongue darted out of the soft ball of cottony fluff. A set of emerald-green eyes blinked back at him.

A kitten.

She—or he—was barely more than the size of a baseball.

"Where'd you come from?"

He received another soft meow in response.

"How'd you do that?" The question came from a husky baritone voice across the way. The shopkeeper from the novelty store stood at the door, staring at Alden in disbelief.

"Do what?"

"My wife and I have been trying to catch that kitten for three days to make sure she's okay. She always gets away. But here you are, and she's practically crawling into your lap."

Huh. Alden shrugged. Darned if he knew why the little critter had chosen to grace him with its presence.

"I don't know. I guess she just likes me."

The man nodded and smiled. "And I would guess you just got yourself a kitten."

CHAPTER FIFTEEN

OLD HABITS WERE hard to break. Hannah had to fight the urge to tell Mama what she wanted to hear. But she was done being conciliatory. At least when it came to her professional life.

"This is a good decision for me, Mama. I need to see if I can make it work," Hannah said into the phone for what had to be the fourth time during their nightly call.

Her mother wasn't thrilled with Hannah's decision to work at a fashion boutique on Newbury Street instead of trying to get her old job back or searching for a comparable one. The boutique had given her a chance after she'd shown them some of her original designs. Eventually, she wanted to work up to displaying her very own creations on the exclusive racks. But the salary was nowhere near as good as what she'd been making as an accountant, a fact that seemed to be keeping her mother up at night.

And unlike before with her past career, now

Hannah felt a spring in her step every time she went into work. She couldn't recall the last time that had ever happened. If ever. And she owed it all to Alden. Hannah would have never attempted to walk into a boutique with a portfolio of designs if it hadn't been for his encouragement and the inspiration that had struck in that fabric store back in Istanbul. Still, it hurt just to think about him. Even with appreciation for the way he'd believed in her talent before she had done so herself.

"But what about all your expenses?" her mother argued, pulling her out of the melancholy thoughts.

"I have a roommate now. So my rent is half of what I used to pay. And I'm finding other ways to cut corners. But right now I have to go." Hannah hung up before her mother could come up with yet another argument.

Said roommate chose that moment to breeze through the door. Lexie gave her a finger wave from across the room. Mandy's sister happened to need a new place to stay because of her recent divorce. The unwelcome acknowledgment that she herself would soon be a divorcee too echoed through her head.

She pushed the thought aside before the ever-ready stinging behind her eyes could start.

She'd done quite enough crying since boarding that plane by herself back in Istanbul.

"Get dressed, Hannah," Lexie said. "You are coming out with us and I'm not taking no for an answer this time."

Not this again.

"I'm really not in the mood. Maybe—"

Lexie held a hand up to stop her. "No arguments. You've done nothing but go to work, then come home and sulk this whole week. Don't make me sorry that I moved in here with you last week."

"I'm already in my pajamas."

Lexie tapped her foot impatiently. "So? You have a closet full of stylish new clothes that fancy boutique is letting you borrow. Go pick something and then make yourself presentable."

"Where are we going?" Hannah asked. Not that it mattered. She didn't want to leave the apartment to go and try to be social. And she certainly didn't want to take the risk that anyone would try and hit on her. She still felt too raw, too vulnerable. Thoughts of Alden kept invading her mind and she would no doubt compare anyone who approached her to her pretend husband. And anyone else was bound to fall woefully short.

"There's a new club over by Fenway. The food and cocktails are supposed to be out of this world. Now, go get dressed so we can see for ourselves."

Hannah made no motion to get up off the couch in the hopes that Lexie might give up on her quest if given enough time. No such luck.

"I'm waiting," Lexie declared, exaggerating the tapping of her foot until Hannah worried the tenants downstairs were going to come knocking on the door to complain.

Hannah sighed with resignation before uncurling her legs from underneath her and standing up. Lexie was clearly not going to let up. "Fine. Just give me a few minutes and I'll go get ready."

Lexie pulled out her phone. "I'll call for a ride share."

Twenty minutes later, they were in a late-model SUV heading toward the center of the city.

She could try to make the best of it. Maybe Lexie was right. Maybe it would do her good to get back out there. She certainly wasn't ready to date again anytime soon. But she could window shop.

The idea fled as soon as she'd thought it. Who was she kidding? Best-case scenario, this night was going to garner a nice meal and a tasty cocktail. Which she wasn't even going to be able to enjoy while she yearned to go back home and crawl into bed. Only to have the blasted dreams invade her sleep.

Dreams of Alden.

Try as she might, she hadn't been able to keep them at bay. They all ended the same way. With him walking away from her as she stood on the sandy beach of a remote island surrounded by turquoise blue water.

Enough.

The club was crowded and loud when they arrived. Hannah stifled a groan once they made it inside. When Lexie dragged her onto the dance floor, she went through the motions as best she could.

The last time she'd danced, she'd been doing her best to mimic the belly dancer as Alden watched her. A rush of heat flooded her cheeks recalling the heat that she'd seen in his eyes then.

Finally, after about ninety minutes, she couldn't fake it any longer.

She leaned into Lexie's ear, doing her best to raise her voice above the noise. "I think I've had my fill. I can make my own way back to the apartment."

"I'll come back with you," Lexie replied.

Great. Now she'd feel guilty for ruining her roommate's evening simply because she was a mopey mess. "It's okay. I'll be fine heading back on my own."

Lexie reached for her arm. "Hannah. I'm coming back with you. We can open up a pint of rocky road and do some girlie chatting."

Hannah couldn't help but feel touched at the other woman's consideration. See? She was going to be fine. She had a friend/roommate who was making sure to get her out of the apartment and then willing to hang with her afterward eating ice cream. She was finally taking a small step toward exploring a new career. Eventually, her broken heart would mend and she would move on even further with her life.

By the time they made it back to their apartment building, she'd almost convinced herself that moving on was possible.

Right up until all the positive thoughts came to a grinding halt. Lexie pointed out the car window as they came to a stop.

"Why is there a man sitting on our stoop?" she asked. "And what's in that big box he's got?"

The woman Hannah stepped out of the car with gave him the most intense glare as they approached. Alden wished he'd purchased a few of those "evil eye" charms to maybe ward off the clear dislike being thrown his way. He vaguely recognized her before placing her as Mandy's older sister.

But he couldn't spare Lexie much thought. His sole focus right now was Hannah. She was utterly, strikingly beautiful. And he'd missed her down to every cell within his body. He could only hope that she might have missed him too. If only a fraction as much.

"Alden? What are you doing here?" She glanced at her watch. "At this time of night, no less."

He'd never considered himself an impulsive man. But lately he hardly recognized himself. And now here he was, following the impulse to see Hannah.

"And what's in that box?" Lexie demanded to know.

He answered Hannah's questions to begin with. "I came to see you about something. And I guess I'm still stuck in that other time zone." He was also hung up back in the time they'd spent together overseas. He hadn't been able to get those moments out of his mind.

"Hello?" Lexie waved a hand at him. "The box?"

"Could we maybe go upstairs? Or even to a café?"

Lexie turned to Hannah, waiting for her to

answer. "It's up to you, Hannah. Whatever you want to do."

As annoying as Alden found the other woman right now, he had to give credit where it was due. Lexie was obviously being protective of her friend. He couldn't begrudge her that.

Hannah hesitated for a split second before nodding her head. "Fine. But you have five minutes. That's it."

He would take it.

Of all the ways she'd imagined running into Alden again, finding him on her doorstep late one night hadn't been one of the possibilities that had come to mind. Now that he was here, she didn't know what she wanted to do more. Throttle him? Or throw herself into his arms and beg him to hold her for just a few moments before she let reality bring her back to her senses.

When they reached the apartment, Lexie used her key to let them all in while Hannah switched the lights on. Her hand shook, her core quivering with the jolt of seeing him again so unexpectedly.

"I'm going to give you both some privacy and go to bed," Lexie said. "Unless you'd like me to stay, Hannah."

As much as she appreciated the offer, she

had to speak to Alden one-on-one. "I'll be fine. Have a good night, Lexie."

"Just promise me you'll tell me the contents of that box tomorrow."

Hannah made the universal motion of crossing her heart. "It's a promise."

She had a sinking feeling she might be able to guess what Alden had brought with him. He apparently couldn't wait any longer to finalize their annulment. Or divorce or whatever it was. She couldn't even be sure at this point. Every time her phone rang since arriving back in Boston, she'd braced herself to speak to one of Alden's attorneys calling to tell her that she was once more officially a single woman.

"Was there no way to do this electronically?" she asked. And couldn't he have found a smaller box for the documents? "Most documents are signed that way these days."

"Signed?"

She pointed to the ground where he'd set the box down. "I'm guessing there are legal papers in there you need my signature on."

Before she got the last word out, she could have sworn she heard a soft mewing noise coming from the floor. And now that she was looking at it carefully, there appeared to be several small holes cut out of the cardboard. Hannah stepped closer to investigate, only to jump back in surprise when the damn thing moved.

"Alden?"

"Yes?"

"What's in there?"

"Where?"

Hannah slammed her hands on her hips. "What is going on, Alden?"

He actually had the nerve to chuckle! "Oh, I brought you something." Leaning down, he lifted the cover. Hannah felt her heart begin to melt when she peered inside. The smallest kitten she'd ever seen sat square in the center, licking its paws and mewing softly.

Without bothering to ask, she reached in and picked it up, bringing the tiny whiskered face closer to hers. A tiny pink tongue darted out and licked her cheek. Hannah's heart was now officially complete mush.

"I don't understand," she began, not able to tear her eyes off the small wiggly bundle she held. "You brought your pet here?"

Alden chuckled. "She's yours. If you want her."

"You're giving her to me?"

He nodded. "Only, I was hoping you might agree to a package deal."

Hannah stood staring at him with her mouth agape for several beats. Alden felt a small pang of guilt for her reaction. Okay, maybe showing up with an adorable kitten was rather unfair. But in his defense, the little creature had approached him first. He'd just wanted to share his feline find with Hannah.

That and so much more. He wanted to share his life with her.

But first he had some groveling to do.

"What kind of package?" Hannah finally asked after a bit more staring.

He stepped closer to her, stroked a finger down her cheek. "One that includes me."

Hannah gasped, her jaw falling farther. She stepped away and gently placed the squirming animal back into the box. Alden pulled a small treat out of his pocket and tossed it in to keep her occupied.

He took both Hannah's hands in his as soon as she straightened. "I was a fool back on the island. There's no way I can make it up to you for how badly I reacted. But please know that I will spend the rest of our lives doing just that."

She blinked at him. "You will?"

He didn't hesitate to answer. "Yes. If you'll let me."

She clasped a hand to her mouth. "Then you're not here to finalize our divorce?"

He had to smile at her confusion. She still didn't seem to be grasping why he'd shown up at her door practically in the middle of the night. He obviously had to make it clearer.

"No, sweetheart. I told you, I'm here to give you the kitten I found in Istanbul. And ask you to take me on as well and, hopefully, any children we might have together. We can buy a family home here in Boston. Or anywhere you want to. As long as we're together. As a family."

"Oh, Alden." The way she said his name sent a wealth of emotion surging through his core. How in the world could he have even considered walking away from this woman?

"Hannah, I love you. I think I may have always loved you. During those high school dances, the homecoming games, and everything in between. And ever since."

Her eyes began to glisten with unshed tears. He could only hope they were happy ones. So he went on. "The smartest thing I ever did was marry you by mistake."

That earned him a small chuckle.

"The dumbest thing I ever did was to think about voiding said marriage," he added. "But luckily I came to my senses with some help from a couple of friends and a wiggly feline."

"How did the cat help?" she asked with an indulgent smile.

He shrugged. "As soon as she nestled up to

me, I knew I had to bring her here and give her to you. She practically told me to."

Hannah laughed. "She did, huh?"

"That's right. She said it was kismet. She also told me to give you this." He reached into his breast pocket, pulled out the ring he'd slipped on her finger what seemed like a decade ago in Vegas.

Taking her hand, he slipped it back on her finger where it belonged. Where it would stay forever if he had anything to say about it.

"Alden, does this mean...?"

He kissed her before she could finish. "I think we should get married again. With a real ceremony this time. As good a job as Elvis did for us, I was thinking something a bit more formal."

"It would be nice if my mom could be there this time."

He stroked her cheek again. Now that she was here in front of him, he couldn't seem to keep his hands off her. He'd never get enough of touching her. Not in this lifetime.

"Your mother. Max and Mandy. Their brothers and sisters." He thrust his thumb in the direction of the bedrooms. "Even Lexie can come if you want her to."

Hannah's laugh sounded like angelic music to his ears. "Thank you. That's very generous."

"We'll have to figure out the best time and ways to get everyone there."

"Get them where? To Boston? That should be easy enough." Further confusion on her part. He was making such a mess of this, but all that mattered was that he was here now. With Hannah.

"Well, I was thinking someplace a bit more exotic. An island in the Mediterranean perhaps."

Her response was to wrap her arms around his neck and snuggle against his cheek.

A loud meowing sound coming from the floor echoed through the air.

"I think she might be getting hungry. Please tell me you have some tuna in the kitchen."

"She can have all the tuna she wants."

"I get the feeling we're going to have a very spoiled little tabby on our hands in a few short weeks."

"I have no doubt. What's her name?" Hannah asked between intermittent sniffles.

"Well, I've been calling her Chunk."

She giggled before answering. "After the cherished cat in Istanbul? Tumbuli."

"You remember, then?"

She nodded. "I remember every cherished moment we spent together, Alden."

Hearing those words shattered the last of his

threadbare control. Alden couldn't hold himself back any longer. Pulling her tighter into his arms, he indulged in the feel of her, thanking his lucky stars that she was ready to give him another chance.

"We don't have to keep that name though," he whispered against her ear. "We can name her something else, if you'd like."

She shook her head, gifted him with a long lingering kiss that made him want to pull her onto the sofa behind them and keep kissing her until neither one of them could catch their breath.

"No," she answered after pulling her mouth off his much too soon. "We'll keep the name. It's perfect. Everything is perfect."

He couldn't agree more.

* * * * *

*If you enjoyed this story,
check out these other great reads
from Nina Singh*

Part of His Royal World
The Prince's Safari Temptation
Two Weeks to Tempt the Tycoon
Caribbean Contract with Her Boss

All available now!

HARLEQUIN
Reader Service

Enjoyed your book?

Try the perfect subscription for Romance readers and get more great books like this delivered right to your door.

See why over 10+ million readers have tried Harlequin Reader Service.

Start with a Free Welcome Collection with free books and a gift—valued over $20.

Choose any series in print or ebook.
See website for details and order today:

TryReaderService.com/subscriptions

RSBPA24R